Bipra

THE MAN

Sarat Chandra Chattopadhyay

Translated from Bengali by

Sukhendu Ray

rota 6 months

at LOU   until...........4/.1..5...

at OAD   until.....................

at LOU   until.....................

NIYOGI
BOOKS

Published by
NIYOGI BOOKS
Block D, Building No. 77,
Okhla Industrial Area, Phase-I,
New Delhi-110 020, INDIA
Tel: 91-11-26816301, 26818960
Email: niyogibooks@gmail.com
Website: www.niyogibooksindia.com

English Text © Sukhendu Ray

Editor: Sukanya Sur
Design: Shraboni Roy

ISBN: 978-93-86906-40-3
Publication: 2018

Printed at: Niyogi Offset Pvt. Ltd., New Delhi, India

For

Jitendra, Ashok, and Sinclair

Translator's Note

Translations are major conduits to spread knowledge and information on various subjects throughout the world. The world has made considerable progress due to the availability of ideas and discoveries by great men and women in translation throughout the past many centuries and in present times.

In our country, from times immemorial, the epics *Ramayana* and *Mahabharata* have been considered as important treatises handed down through generations, initially by oral narrations and subsequently in translations in diverse Indian languages. The original language of both these epics was Sanskrit, which was accessible to only a few scholarly persons, and hence the many translations in various Indian languages.

Bipradas is regarded as one of the best works of Sarat Chandra Chattopadhyay. This book is perhaps somewhat offbeat in terms of Sarat Chandra's usual métier. The theme of *Bipradas* is a conflict of cultures—ancient Indian Hindu culture versus the modern culture, influenced mainly by western culture, western education, and reformatory ideas.

Bipradas, the protagonist of this novel, is unique. He is young and handsome, physically strong, of powerful moral fibre, and a most determined character not amenable to unprincipled compromises.

Although held by all in great respect and awe, he is compassionate by nature.

By all accounts, he is a supremely rational man; yet he believes in orthodox Hindu culture and its rituals, including caste system and contamination by touch. Though he did not have much formal education, he happens to be extremely well educated with wide reading. He efficiently manages the affairs of his vast estate as well as the family, and his style of management is often regarded as autocratic.

Then arrives Bandana, the cousin of Bipradas's wife Sati, and conflict follows. Bandana is a young girl of the new age and well-cultivated. She lives in Bombay with her father and leads a Western lifestyle. They consider conservative Hindu rituals abhorrent and unacceptable. She is revolted when she discovers that no one in Bipradas's family would drink water or eat food offered by her father or herself. Apparently, they are considered untouchables!

Surprisingly, or perhaps not so surprisingly, living for a time with this archly orthodox family makes Bandana curious about how such ancient rites and rituals keep the family together. Progressively, Bandana comes to appreciate these rituals, almost to the point of becoming a convert. She is vastly attracted by Bipradas—his personality, his intellect, and the courage of his conviction.

A tragedy then strikes the family. Bipradas falls out with his sister's husband Sasadhar, whom he accuses of cheating him, and asks Sasadhar to leave his home. Dayamoyee intervenes and disagrees to abandon her son-in-law. As a result, it is Bipradas who leaves home with his wife and child, practically penniless.

Shortly thereafter, Sati dies while in exile, and Bipradas returns home for his son to perform his mother's funeral rites. On a piteous appeal from Dwijadas, Bandana promptly arrives to hold the reins of a disarrayed home. She agrees to marry Dwijadas with Bipradas's consent, and begs Bipradas to let her keep his son with her. Having renounced the worldly life, Bipradas soon leaves home, and with him goes his mother Dayamoyee on a pilgrimage. Dayamoyee would return home sooner or later, but never would Bipradas.

Translation from one language to another is always arduous, since no two languages are truly equivalent in anything except the simplest terms. There was no way in spite of my best efforts to match my translation with the elegant Bengali of Sarat Chandra. I had thought it right to be as faithful to the original text as was possible. Some liberties had to be taken where translations did not convey with any degree of fidelity the nuances of the original language. Such liberties have been minimal.

The text adopted in this translation is taken from Sarat Chandra's collected works published by Sarat Samity.

I am, as usual, deeply grateful to my wife Bharati for all her help and encouragement. I am also indebted to Mr Nirmal Kanti Bhattacharjee for his help.

January 2018   **Sukhendu Ray**

ONE

It was a Sunday morning in the village of Balarampur. A meeting of the peasants had just ended in the village commons. The status of the meeting had been elevated somewhat by the participation of railway porters from the nearby railway colony. Seasoned speakers from Calcutta addressed the meeting with fiery speeches, sprouting the usual slogans of inequality and poor treatment of the peasants. After the meeting ended, the participants marched through the village.

As villages go, Balarampur was comparatively prosperous, comprising a number of large and small landholders and a few well-off families. Different communities had their own earmarked settlements and lived in cottages.

The richest family was the local zamindar, who, over generations, had built a substantial fortune through the judicious acquisition of land, while engaging in moneylending on the side. As the procession winding through the village approached the huge mansion of the zamindar, a tall and well-built young man watched the goings-on below with amused interest from the balcony of the first floor. Upon sighting him, the tumultuous noise created by the crowd instantly died down. Following the gaze of some of the people, the leaders at the head of the procession spotted the young man who quickly slipped behind a pillar.

'Who is he?' they asked.

Many answered, 'Bipradasbabu.'

'Who is this Bipradas? Is he the zamindar?'

'Yes, he is,' someone confirmed.

Being from the city, the leaders were no respecters of personages. 'O, just that,' they contemptuously observed. They called for another round of vituperative slogan-shouting to which they did not receive much of a response. Feeling slighted, the leaders sneered, 'Scared of a petty village zamindar? They are our worst enemy, the blood-sucking leeches!'

The rousing condemnations were suddenly interrupted. They had many more invectives in their armoury that remained unexpressed because of the interruption. Someone in the crowd said quietly, 'He happens to be his elder brother.'

'Whose?'

A young man of about twenty-five, who was carrying a banner at the head of the procession, detached himself from the crowd and said, 'Mine.' It was that young man's generous funding and keen interest that had made it possible to hold the day's meeting successfully.

'Yours? Do you also happen to be a zamindar of this village?'

The young man did not respond.

TWO

The following day, Bipradas met his younger brother in his room.

'Your show yesterday went off fairly well. Very striking, I must say. The war cries were well chosen and sharp, I must admit.'

Dwijadas remained standing quietly.

Bipradas asked, 'Did this procession of yours pass deliberately under my nose in order to scare me?'

Dwijadas replied demurely, 'No, it was not just for you. Regardless of the route a procession takes, those who have reasons to fear will be afraid.'

Bipradas hid a smile. His brother was so full of disdain. Then he said, 'Many amongst your demonstrators know the nature of your brother, or else I need not have gone to the balcony to hear them shouting. I could have easily done that from my room. Your banners and tirades do not put me off. I am well aware that with artificial teeth, one may be able to grimace frighteningly, but one cannot bite.'

What silenced many at yesterday's demonstration was no secret, and Dwijadas felt mortified that his brother hinted at it. By nature, Dwijadas was a quiet and gentle person and, since he held his elder brother in great esteem, he usually avoided getting into any arguments with him. But he found his brother's gibe difficult to stomach. He protested gently, 'Dada, we are aware of the limitations of artificial teeth; but there are people in this world with real teeth who will not hesitate to bite when the need arises.'

At that unexpected rejoinder from Dwijadas, Bipradas looked at him in surprise and said, 'Indeed!'

Dwijadas was about to reply, but stopped short out of fear. Not for fear of his brother, but of his mother whose voice was heard from outside the room.

'Why must you hang curtains on the doors? There is no way that I can come in without touching them. Both our home and lifestyle are getting progressively anglicized.'

Dwijadas rose promptly and pulled the curtains apart. Bipradas also rose from his chair. A middle-aged, widowed lady who still retained her good looks entered the room. She was somewhat lean, with the austerities of widowhood deeply etched on her face. Facing her elder son, with her younger son behind her, she said, 'I say, Bipin. I believe there is some confusion about the date of the ekadasi this month. That never happens.'

'There shouldn't be,' observed Bipradas.

'Please send for Smritiratnamashai. Let's have his opinion.'

With a little smile, Bipradas said, 'I shall do so, but how does it matter what he thinks? Now that you have heard about this,

I am sure you will observe both the alleged dates and not allow even a drop of water to pass through your lips.'

'Does anyone deliberately fast on a whim?' Dayamoyee asked. 'But what can one do? There may not be any virtue in fasting; but if you don't, you are consigned to eternal perdition. By the way, Bouma tells me that she has read in the newspaper about an eminent scholar in Calcutta, who has been preaching some wonderful sermons from the Gita. Can you find out if he would agree to visit and talk to us?'

'Certainly, if you tell me to.'

'But why must I tell you? Are you also not interested? It has been so long since we had a sermonizer visit us.'

'Please, Mother, it has not even been three months since then.'

'Only three months? But that is still long enough. In any event, you cannot say no to what I am going to ask you now. My two aunts have just written, proposing a visit to Kailashnath and Mansarovar. I am determined to go with them.'

Bipradas appealed to her with folded hands, 'For God's sake, Mother, do not ask me to agree to this. I cannot allow you to travel to Tibet in the care of only your aunts, unless accompanied by one of your sons. I am prepared to suffer any losses, but not the loss of my mother.'

Softened by his concern for her, Dayamoyee comforted her son, 'Do not worry about your mother. She doesn't have enough accumulated virtue to be fortunate enough to die on the way to Kailash. I will safely return. It is your responsibility to look after the affairs of our estate and this large home, and I am afraid

I cannot agree to go even to heaven with my other son. Despite being the child of a conservative Brahmin home, he observes none of the usual rituals, and there are reports that in Calcutta, he indulges in prohibited food. On top of that, have you heard what he did yesterday?'

Feigning ignorance, Bipradas asked, 'What did he do? I haven't heard anything.'

'That's not possible,' Dayamoyee sounded sceptical. 'That boy does not have the gumption to do anything without your knowledge. My money supports him, yet he spends all of it to get people from Calcutta to incite my tenants against me. You should stop his Calcutta allowance.'

Bipradas was taken aback. 'What are you saying, Mother? Not pay for his education? You do not want him to study?'

Dayamoyee replied, 'What is the need for that? Have you forgotten that episode when a bunch of students from my father-in-law's school came protesting that the foreign system of education was ruining our country? You became furious and chased them away. Now that your own brother propagates the same idea, should you not act? How do you justify this?'

Bipradas answered, 'There is an explanation, Mother. I cannot stomach it when schoolboys who have failed come complaining, but it does not bother me when someone like Diju, who has a master's degree, condemns foreign education.'

'But what about when he uses my money and incites my tenants against me?' Dayamoyee queried.

Dwijadas, who had remained quiet until then, spoke up, 'Not

a single penny was spent from your estate for yesterday's rally.'

She had not looked behind her since she had entered the room, and she did not do so even then. It was to Bipradas she turned. 'Ask that wretched boy how he got the money? Did he earn it?'

Just then, the sound of tinkling bangles could be heard through the curtains. Bipradas listened attentively and said, 'Ah, there is your answer, Mother. If your own daughter-in-law provides the money, who is going to stop it?'

Dayamoyee then understood and said, 'That's it, isn't it? It is all Sati's doing! I had forgotten that as a rich man's daughter, she receives an annual allowance of six thousand rupees. And it is she who gives money to her precious brother-in-law.'

After a pause, she resumed, 'When your father-in-law came seeking you as the groom, I discouraged marriage to a girl from that family. One Anath Ray of that family went to England and returned with an English wife. There is nothing too outrageous for them.'

Bipradas smiled, but said nothing. He well knew that poor Sati would never be free of that stigma. Mother could never forget that some Anath Ray from her family had married a westernized Bengali woman.

Observing that everyone had gone quiet, she relented and said, 'Let us leave it for now. Kailashnath is calling me. I will settle this issue when I return.' Then she left.

Bipradas spoke to Dwijadas, 'I say, Diju, will you be able to go with her? Now that she has made up her mind, it will not be easy to deter her.'

Dwijadas immediately refused and said, 'You know, Dada,

that I have no faith in the divine. At any rate, you did hear her say that she was not prepared to travel with me even to heaven.'

Bipradas felt exasperated.

'Yes, O Wise One, I heard her. But just tell me if you can go with her or not.'

'I am sorry. I am far too busy now.' With those words, Dwijadas left to avoid further interrogation.

Bipradas sighed, 'I see. You are too busy with your work for the nation to spare any time for your mother.'

Dayamoyee was not Bipradas's real mother, but his stepmother. Within a year of Bipradas's own mother's death, his father Jajneshwar married Dayamoyee and she had raised Bipradas from that time. Bipradas had learnt about this only after he had grown up.

THREE

Of all the people in the house, Dwijadas had the highest regard for his boudie. The money for all his unnecessary expenditures came from her. Sati was not just his senior in terms of their relationship, but also older by a few months. So Sati often called Dwijadas by his name, and it had made Dwijadas run to his mother when he was a child, complaining about Sati's indiscretion.

Sati had arrived in the family when she was a mere child of nine, and so was hugely spoilt. Her mother-in-law had smiled at Dwijadas's complaint and asked, 'Is it true, Bouma? It is not at all proper to call your brother-in-law by name.'

Sati retaliated, 'Why not? I am much older than him!'

'Much older? How much?'

'I was born in the month of Baisakh, and he in the month of Bhadra.'

Dayamoyee smiled indulgently and told her, 'Yes, in the month of Bhadra—I had forgotten this myself. If he comes griping to me again, I will pull his ears.'

Having lost his case in his court of appeal, Dwijadas left sullenly. The mother-in-law drew the daughter-in-law close to her and spoke affectionately, 'He is a child, so he does not always understand. It makes him immensely happy to be called Thakurpo. Do call him so occasionally.'

Sati had nodded her head in agreement, 'Yes, Ma, I will do so.'

About a fortnight after the proposal for Dwijadas to escort his mother to her contemplated visit to Kailashnath was mooted, Sati entered her brother-in-law's study and said, 'I say, Thakurpo...'

Dwijadas raised his hand to stop her. 'That will do, Boudie. No need to butter me up. I will do what you wish me to.'

'What will you do?'

'Whatever you ask me to do. But this is very wrong of Dada.'

'Why?'

Still piqued, Dwijadas said, 'I know everything. I just passed Dada's room. In there, Ma, Dada, and you were hatching a plot against me, but they dare not speak to me and so they got you to do their foul work. Isn't that perverse?'

With a smile, Sati said, 'Not at all, Thakurpo. They know well that as soon as they ask you, you will immediately excuse yourself on the pretext of having no time to spare. But Diju cannot say no if Boudie asks him.'

'Yes, that is my weakness and their strength. What is it you want me to do?'

'Ma is determined to visit Kailashnath, and you will have to go with her.'

After a little pause, Dwijadas said, 'It will be for at least two to three months. Do you realize how my work will suffer?'

Sati accepted that there would be some loss and then said, 'But look at the bright side. You will see a new place, and there will be something to be gained from that. Please, I implore you, don't say no.'

Dwijadas agreed, 'Fine, I will go because you ask me. But did you hear when Ma very calmly asked Dada to stop paying for my study in Calcutta?'

Sati smiled it away, 'Ah, that was because she was peeved, but do remember that the decision to pay for your education was made by none other than Ma.'

Dwijadas replied, 'It is unlikely that I could forget it, but since then, I have also made a decision of my own. Shall I tell you? I am a single man, all alone. My needs are not much. If the occasion ever rises, I can take up the private coaching of students; but I will never ask for a penny from the estate.'

Sati waved it away, 'You will never have to ask, Thakurpo. It will come to you unasked. Even if that fails, you will still not need to coach students—not as long as I am alive. That will be my responsibility.'

Dwijadas accepted that as the axiomatic truth. For an instant, he was emotionally stirred, but quickly recovering, he asked, 'Has the date of her departure been fixed yet? It is strange that I have to accompany her! She firmly declared that day that she was not prepared to even go to heaven with a non-believer like me. What a very curious turn of fate, is it not?'

Sati kept quiet.

'That does not matter,' Diju said, 'I will never disobey you, Boudie. You can assure them of that.'

Sati smiled, 'They were pretty relieved once they dispatched me to you. As soon as I came out of their room, I heard your dada confidently telling Ma to go ahead and make arrangements for her journey without any anxiety. He said, "My brother will not dare to get into any arguments with our emissary. He will listen to her like an obedient boy. Of that I am confident."'

Dwijadas resented it and, after a moment, he said, 'If they deliberately schemed to make me the vehicle to satisfy a lady's meaningless whims, do tell them on my behalf that they should be ashamed of themselves.'

'It will be totally useless, Thakurpo. It is the policy of zamindars to suck the blood of their tenants. They stop at nothing to get their work done, and suffer no regrets. It makes me sad when you hesitate to take any money from the estate, even though half of it is yours, and yet it also pleases me immensely. I have assured Ma on your behalf that there will be no impediments to her trip and that you will go with her. Do return safely from this pilgrimage, and I promise to compensate you for all your losses.'

Dwijadas got up from his chair, touched his boudie's feet, and again took his seat.

'Thus far, I have been advocating the cause of others, but now I need to plead my own,' said Sati.

Dwijadas laughed, 'Your own? No, Boudie, I can't help you there.'

Sati joined in the laughter, 'I am not surprised, Thakurpo. But I am worried that you may say no after hearing me out.'

'Well, try me.'

'I have an uncle, a cousin of my father's, who, because he travelled to England, is an outcaste in the family. Had your people known about this before my marriage, I would have never been accepted by them. I presume you have heard this story from Ma.'

'Again and again. Assuming, on an average, that I have heard this story at least once each day, it probably adds up to five or six thousand times by now.'

'That would be my guess as well. My uncle lives in Bombay. His only daughter studies there at present. I believe she plans to travel to England next year for further studies. I'd like you to escort her here.'

'From Bombay?'

'Yes, from Bombay. She says she can travel alone, but it is so far that I dare not let her travel alone.'

'But why me? Does she not have anyone who can accompany her here?'

'No, my uncle will not get leave from work to come with her.'

Dwijadas didn't know how he could make that commitment. Sati continued, 'She was a little girl of seven or eight years when I was married, and I saw her only once when she matriculated and started college—that was so many years ago. I am very fond of her. In her letters, she has told me how much she wanted to visit us, but I could never find an appropriate occasion. If only you could bring her here.'

Dwijadas asked, 'But what is this appropriate occasion now? Has Ma agreed?'

Sati could not answer him directly and looked anxious. She said hesitantly, 'Yes, I have spoken to Ma, but she has not said anything yet. She seems to be preoccupied with her forthcoming pilgrimage, which makes me hope that she will not object. At any rate, since Ma will not be here for about three months, my sister can easily visit us then.'

It became clear to Dwijadas that though Sati had not received her mother-in-law's consent, she wished to take advantage of her mother-in-law's absence to get her sister to visit her.

Dwijadas asked, 'Do they belong to the Brahmo sect?'

Sati shook her head, 'No, they do not, but Hindu society does not accept them as their own either. I do not think they know where they stand. And that is how it goes.'

That was the situation of most people. Though not quite happy about it, Dwijadas said, 'Well, I am willing to travel to Bombay, but I suggest that you do not bring her when Ma is here. You know Ma. She will create such a fuss about food, pollution by touch, and other things that will make you very embarrassed with your sister here. It is better that she comes here while we are away.'

Sati accepted it as sound advice; but since she had invited them herself, she was unsure how to take the invitation back in the face of this uncertainty.

Sati continued, 'I am not saying this because she is my sister, Thakurpo. Once when I spent a month in Calcutta with her, I found her to be a rare girl in terms of both looks and accomplishmens. Whatever be their general lifestyle, if Ma watches her closely for a couple of days, her ideas about an unorthodox woman will change radically.'

'But, Boudie, you will find it very difficult to get Ma observe her for two days. She will just refuse to do so.'

'Ma will surely see how beautiful she is. She can hardly deny that. My sister is noted for her looks. I am firm in my belief that no one on earth can ignore Bandana—not even Ma.'

Dwijadas looked surprised. 'Bandana? Is that her name? I believe I have heard this name in some context or the other. Perhaps, I have seen her somewhere. Ah, wait, I think there was a picture of her in the newspaper...'

Before he finished speaking, a maid came in and said, 'Ah, here you are, Bouma. An uncle of yours has arrived with his daughter from Bombay. There is no one at home, not even Barababu. The manager has taken them to the ground-floor sitting room.'

It was most unexpected. 'What? What did you say?' Sati rushed out of the room, followed by Dwijadas.

FOUR

A middle-aged gentleman, immaculately clad in European clothes, was sitting on an armchair, and standing near him was a girl of around twenty-one, who, at that moment, was looking intently at a picture of Goddess Jagadhatri that hung on the wall. Her dress, though not western, did not quite conform to the usual attire of Indian women. Her complexion was unusually fair, almost white, which was uncommon for Bengali women. She was slim and her face radiated beauty. Sati's claim that even her mother-in-law would not be able to deny her beauty once she laid her eyes on her sister was not an idle boast.

Sati came into the room and went straight to her uncle. After touching his feet, she said, 'Uncle, have you finally remembered your niece?'

The gentleman stood up, affectionately put his hand on Sati's head, and said, 'Yes, child, I have. But when did you ever invite me that I could have ignored you? Now that I am here without invitation, you are making a show of protest.'

Spotting Dwijadas, he asked who he was.

Sati said, 'Oh, him? He is Diju, my brother-in-law.' Dwijadas greeted him formally with folded hands.

Bandana touched Sati's feet, then laughed and said, 'Ah, so this is the precious character whose subversive activities are a constant threat to the stability of this large estate. I gathered this from your letter. I believe that he is a staunch nationalist, totally alienated from the culture of his family and clan.'

'When did I write all this to you?'

'Only the other day. How can you forget?'

'No, I did not write all that. You are making a mistake.'

Until then, Dwijadas had been sitting rigid with discomfort. He had no idea how to conduct himself in the presence of young women to whom he was not related. There had been no occasion to do so in the past. But he admired the free and easy manners of the new young woman. He shrugged off his discomfort and was filled with pleasure. Intellectually, he had always been an advocate of women's emancipation and education and believed that it was wrong to keep them unlettered and confined to the home. That paradigmatic young woman guest confirmed his belief.

Speaking to the young woman, he said, 'You are right. It is possible that what Boudie wrote may have escaped her mind. But let us put this behind us.' Then he turned to Sati and said, 'You know very well that your strength is the source of my strength, and yet you write all this about me. Fine. If all of you wish to disown me, go ahead. I will renounce all my rights to the property. Let your estate prosper perennially. You just have to say the word and I will get a lawyer and give up my rights in writing. Try me.'

Raysahib looked up and asked, 'Is your brother-in-law a very committed nationalist?'

'Rabidly so,' answered Sati.

'And is it also true that if you ask, he will unhesitatingly sacrifice his share in the property?'

Sati nodded her head and said, 'Quite easily. There is nothing that he cannot do.'

Bandana was intrigued. She asked him, 'Is it really true that you can renounce your rights for life?'

'Yes, I can, I truly can. I have no interest, none at all, in this property. Ninety per cent of our people do not get to eat even one square meal a day despite doing back-breaking labour all day long, and here I am served with the best of food without having to lift a finger. I have no stomach for such iniquitous food. I can in no way swallow that food. It is better to be unshackled by wealth. I will be happy to live the way that most of our people do. If I can earn my bread, well and good; if not, I can starve to death like the rest of them. That way, it will perhaps be easier to gain heaven than with my present lifestyle.'

Bandana was listening to him spellbound.

Sati said, 'This is Thakurpo's standard spiel. He repeats it so many times that he seems to have memorized it. That is enough for now, Thakurpo. You will have plenty of time to deliver your old lectures later. My uncle hasn't even had a moment to freshen up. Come, Bandana, let us go up and you can change your clothes.'

Raysahib asked, 'But where is our son-in-law? I have not met him yet.'

'He is out on some work and may be returning late,' Sati replied.

Bandana asked, 'We have not met your mother-in-law either. Is she at home?'

'Yes, she is. She spends almost the entire morning with her pujas. You will see her later in the day.'

'Does she keep busy mainly with her devotional activities?' asked Bandana.

'Yes, she does.'

'After her widowhood, I believe, she has not taken much interest in running the home.'

'Yes, it is true. It is left to me now to look after everything.'

Bandana asked with a touch of curiosity, 'Is it true that she is your stepmother-in-law?'

Sati laughed, 'Frankly, I do not know. After all, I never saw my own mother-in-law.'

Dwijadas chipped in, 'It isn't true. Does it mean that your stepmother-in-law is Dada's stepmother? No. She is a stepmother all right—but mine, not Dada's. Let it go now. We can talk about it when we all have freshened up. Boudie, don't waste any more time. Take them upstairs.'

He was on his way to see to the arrangements for the visitors when he was stopped in his tracks by his mother.

Possibly informed about the unexpected visitors, Dayamoyee had left her puja and come out. As she was not that old, post her widowhood, she used to talk to men who were not relatives from behind screens. However, on that day, she came openly into the room. Her head was covered only down to her brows, her face entirely uncovered.

'My sejokaka and my sister Bandana,' Sati said by way of introduction. Then, unexpectedly, Sati touched her mother-in-law's feet. It was not usual in the circumstances. Dayamoyee, somewhat surprised, affectionately touched her chin and blessed her. Her eyes hardened as soon as she spotted Bandana. Following her didi, Bandana bent down to touch her feet, but Dayamoyee did not allow it and stepped back, perhaps to avoid getting touched by her. She just said softly, 'Live long.' Addressing the gentleman, she said, 'Namaskar, Beimashai, our children are indeed fortunate for your unexpected visit.'

The gentleman, reciprocating her greeting, said, 'Benthakrun, the pressure of work does not leave me enough time for my social obligations. Please do forgive us for arriving without notice, but for our next visit, we shall certainly let you know well in advance.'

Dayamoyee did not respond to his words. She merely said, 'Sadly, my pujas are not yet over, so we will meet later. Bouma, take them up and see to their food. Do ask Bipin to see me when he comes.' Then she left without another word. On the face of it, nothing was wrong with the formal courtesies, but privately, they all felt that there was a hint of a passing cloud in an otherwise clear sky.

FIVE

After taking her bath and changing her clothes, Bandana returned to the sitting room to find her father freshened up, occupying a majestic easy chair and reading a newspaper. On a side table lay stacks of newspapers, and Dwijadas was busy sorting them out in sequence. What with the long railway journey and other work, Sati's uncle had missed out on reading the newspapers. When he observed his daughter, he said, 'Child, we will catch the 2:00 p.m. train to Calcutta. If you wish to stay for a while with your didi, then I shall leave you here and proceed straight to Bombay. How do you feel about this?'

'How long will you be in Calcutta, Baba?'

'May be for about eight days, but not more.'

'Who will then take me to Bombay?'

'That may not be difficult to fix,' he said, 'but if you so wish, you can remain here for a few days and, on my way to Bombay, I will collect you.'

Bandana mused and then said, 'Let me check with Mejdi.'

Dwijadas said, 'Boudie is in the kitchen; she might be late.' Then, pointing to the bundle of newspapers in his hand, he asked Bandana, 'Which newspaper is your choice?'

'Newspapers? I don't read them.'

'You don't read newspapers?'

'No, I have no patience for that. In the evening, I listen to Father's stories, and that is good enough for me.'

'Strange! I believed you read a great deal.'

'Since you do not know anything about me, what makes you think that? That is rather odd, is it not?'

Finding him embarrassed, Bandana smiled and said, 'I have no interest in reading about how much freedom you have all achieved for the nation and how furious the British have been because of it. But my father is. He gets lost in newspapers and becomes dead to the outside world.'

Bandana's father probably heard his daughter referring to him and, without taking his eyes off the paper he was reading, said, 'Just a minute—ah—this is the response I was looking for.'

With a little smile on her face, she said, 'Fine, Baba, go ahead and scan the newspapers as long as you wish. I am in no hurry.' Then, looking at Dwijadas, she said, 'Didi tells me that you have a great library. Can we go there and see your collection?'

'Certainly, let me take you there.'

The library was on the second floor. While climbing up the broad steps, Dwijadas said, 'The library is fairly large, except that it is not mine but my dada's. My job is to hunt for new publications and procure them as Dada wishes.'

'But surely you read them?'

'Nothing to speak of. The reader is the owner of the library. He is full of energy and is gifted with an exceptional intellect.

'Who? Your dada?'

'Yes. He may not have the pedigree of a university education, but I do believe that there is no equal in our country to his impressive erudition. But have you not ever met your brother-in-law?'

'No, tell me what does he look like?'

'Just my opposite—like day and night. I am dark, but he has a golden complexion. He is well known in our neighbourhood for his physical prowess. His skill with guns, swords, and lathis is unparalled. Other than Mother, no one has the courage to look him in the face and speak to him.'

'Not even my mejdi?' asked Bandana.

'No, not even her.'

'Is he very ill-tempered?'

'No, he is not. There is a word in English language— "aristocrat". I have a feeling that in some past birth, my dada must have been their king. You asked if he was ill-tempered, but he has hardly any occasion to be so.'

'You have a strong devotion for your dada, is it not?' Bandana asked.

Dwijadas remained quiet for some time and then said, 'If it is ever possible for me to give an answer to your question, I will do so then.'

Bandana looked nonplussed and said, 'What do you mean by that?'

With a little laugh, Dwijadas said, 'If I told you what I meant now, then I would not have to wait to give you my reply later. So let it be.'

The library was fairly large. It was expensively furnished, well equipped, and neatly arranged. She was amazed at finding such a library in a village. In a big city like Bombay, libraries like this were commonplace, but living in a village and creating such a collection just for one's own needs was indeed most astonishing. Bandana asked, 'Does your dada read all these books?'

Dwijadas answered, 'He does and he has. The shelves are not locked. Pick up any book and scan it. You are sure to find signs that he has read it.'

'How does he find the time? Does he read all the time, day and night?'

Dwijadas shook his head. 'I don't think so. Our property may not be large, but it is not small either. Dada has to keep an eye on all its affairs. It is nothing new; our father had planned all that during his lifetime. Like you, I am also mystified as to how he finds time for all that he does. It is my belief that occasionally we come across rare individuals who are outside the realm of normal people, and my dada is that kind of person. They do not read painstakingly like we do; they grasp the essence simply by running their eyes over the printed words. But enough of my dada now. You have not met him yet, and my one-sided talk about him may sound exaggerated.'

'I like it.'

'But simply liking it is not enough. There are many ordinary people like us; if one extraordinary person continues to pervade all our thoughts, then where will that leave us? God did not give us voices just to sing hymns of praise for others.'

'Meaning that leaving Dada aside, it is time now to sing hymns for the younger brother—that is what you mean, is it not?' teased Bandana.

Diju smiled and said, 'Yes, indeed, that is what I want. But where is the scope for that? Those who know me will not care; those who do not may have only a passing interest in doing so. Not being used to it, I may fumble singing my own hymn.'

Bandana encouraged him, 'No, you won't. Give it a shot. I believe that men are born good at it. So, don't waste time. Start now.'

'No, I cannot do it. I'd rather you look at some of the books. I will go and send Boudie up.'

Just as he was about to go, Bandana said assertively, 'What a fine man you are! No, you cannot leave me alone here. I have read enough. I don't need to read anymore. It is better that you talk and I listen.'

'Talk about what?'

'About yourself.'

'Well, in that case, I'd better go down and send you a much better speaker.'

'Meaning Mejdi, isn't it? She has said whatever she had to in her letters. What I want to know is if that is true.'

'It is not; not at least seventy-five per cent of it. Well, is it true that you are planning to go to England?'

It became clear that the man was unwilling to talk about himself, and it would be indecorous to press him further, as though they were very close. She said, 'It is my father's wish. He wants me to finish my schooling there. Why don't you come as well?'

'I am open to it, but where would I get the money for that? I cannot depend on my ability to earn by coaching students there, and neither can I put this burden on Boudie. So that is the way it is. I cannot go.'

Bandana was amused. 'You are talking out of pique. With your present wealth, you can take, in addition to yourself, half the village people with you, if you wish. I will make all the arrangements, and all you have to do is to be ready to go.'

Dwijadas said, 'That is not to be. It is true that there is no shortage of funds, but all that belongs to Dada and not to me. It will perhaps not be an overstatement to say that I live on charity.'

In her effort to dismiss that by laughing it away, Bandana said, 'I do have the sense to understand what is exaggeration and what is not, but this is once again due to your resentment. I recall Mejdi writing that you are unwilling to accept property that you have not earned. Is that so?'

Diju said, 'If it were true, it would be because of one's moral code and not indignation. But it is not entirely so.'

'What is the truth then?'

Dwijadas kept quiet. Bandana, looking at him, spoke softly, 'I am not curious by nature, and I realize that this curiosity of mine is immoderate. Nevertheless, it still does not satisfy me. On the contrary, I have heard so much about you that when we first met, you did not seem to be a stranger at all. I recognized you so easily, as if I had known you for a long time. If you can talk to Mejdi so freely about yourself, then why not to me as well? In a way, I am sort of a relation.'

Dwijadas was both embarrassed and discomfitted as he listened to her. It was the very first time he had had such a long conversation with an adult woman who was a stranger to him. He looked at the wall clock and realized that they had been talking for more than an hour. Had someone been looking for them in the meantime, he would not know what to say. Perhaps, his dada had returned home or his mother had completed her prayers. His mind and body felt restless, as if desiring to dash towards the staircase; but unable to move, he simply sat there.

 Bandana said, 'But you have told me nothing. Tell me something, please.'

Diju came out of his reverie and said, 'If I were to tell you, then you would be the first person to hear what I am about to say. I have not even told Boudie.'

'That is between you and your boudie to settle, but I am not leaving without....'

Diju knew that he ought not to say anything, but he found it difficult to ignore Bandana's curiosity. Finally, he said, 'My father in fact left me nothing.'

Bandana appeared stunned. 'What? That can't be true! It is just not possible!'

'Yes, it is true.'

'But why?'

'Father was afraid that in my hands, his property might go down the drain.'

'Was there any basis for such fear?'

'There was. Once he lost a lot of money just to save me.'

Bandana recalled a hint of something like that in one of Sati's letters. She asked, 'Did your father leave a will?'

'Only Dada knows. He says no if I ask him.'

With a deep sigh, Bandana said, 'That's a relief. I thought he deprived you of everthing in his will.'

Dwijadas said, 'It was not that my father was unwilling to do so, but I believe Dada prevented it.'

'Your dada prevented it! How very odd!'

Diju said with a grin, 'If you knew my dada, you would not think it odd. It was around evening one day. The servants had still not lit the lamps. I was in the next room looking for a book when I caught my father's voice. I heard my dada say "no", but Father kept insisting, "Why not, Bipradas? I cannot allow my ancestral property to go to ruin. I will find no peace even when I am gone." But Dada was firm, "This can in no way be proper." Father replied, "In that case, I will leave everything in your hands, and if you feel he deserves it, let him have his share, otherwise not." Father was still alive two or three years after that, but I know for sure that he did not change his mind.'

'Does anyone else know this?' asked Bandana.

'No, no one. I know this because I overheard it.'

After being pensive for a while, Bandana commented, 'Your dada is truly an extraordinary character.'

'Yes, he is, but I ought to go now. I am already late. You can stay here and read until you are summoned.'

'I have no desire to read now. As I will be here for a few days, there will be ample time for reading.'

Dwijadas was about to leave when he stopped and asked, 'Are you not travelling to Calcutta with your father?'

'No. I will return to Bombay with him when he comes back from Calcutta.'

'I'd suggest that you stay back here for a few days during that time.'

'That was our original plan, but there are certain snags. There is no one who can accompany me to Bombay. If you agree to do so, I can accept your suggestion.'

'But I shan't be here then. I will be accompanying Mother on her pilgrimage to Kailash next Monday.'

'To Kailash? I believe that is a glorious sight!' Bandana's eyes shone brightly. 'Who else is going with you?'

'I really do not know, but I believe that there will be a few people.'

'Will you take me with you?'

Dwijadas was silent. Hurt, Bandana tried to laugh it off and said, 'Ah, that is why you gave me your wonderful advice to stay here while you will be away.'

Dwijadas replied calmly, 'In a sense, you are right. Boudie has told you so much about us in her letters, but did she never tell you how very orthodox our family is? Had she never hinted at the strictness of our life?'

'No.'

'No? That is surprising.' Dwijadas pondered briefly and then said, 'Do you know that no one in this home, but I, will drink water from your hand?'

'Dada?'

'No.'

'Mejdi?'

'Not even she.'

Shaken, Bandana asked, 'Is it really true?'

'It is. Absolutely.'

Just then, Sati's voice was heard from down the staircase, 'Thakurpo, Bandana, what are you two busy at?'

'We will be with you soon.' Dwijadas was about to leave when Bandana, her face ashen, said, 'I did not know all this. Thank you for telling me.'

SIX

Going downstairs, Bandana found her father happily having his lunch. On a small table in the sitting room, food had been served on silver plates. A tall and handsome person was standing near the table. From his strong physique and fair complexion, Bandana correctly inferred that he must be Bipradas. Sati did not enter the room, but she confirmed that the person was indeed Bipradas and suggested that she touch his feet.

This is something that Bengali girls need not be taught. The way she had earlier paid her homage to Dayamoyee, she could have easily done the same to her brother-in-law, but somehow the idea repelled her. For the sake of her sister, she folded her hands and greeted him, but the gesture accentuated her disregard. She spoke to her father, 'Why are you eating alone? You could have sent for me.'

Her father looked up and said, 'I have to catch a train, but you do not have to rush. After I leave, you all can take your time and eat comfortably.'

From outside the room, Sati indicated her approval by nodding. Addressing her, Bandana said, 'Mejdi, you could have served food to Father on enamel or chinaware instead of ruining so many silver plates.'

Raysahib stopped eating. Being simple-minded, he did not quite grasp the significance of his daughter's remark, so feeling embarrassed—as if it were his fault—he said, 'Really, really, I did not notice this—ah, Sati where are you? You could have used ordinary plates.'

Bipradas was outraged by the audacity of this chit of a girl. No one in his life had dared so far to affront him as this kinswoman, who had just arrived, had. Her anxiety about silverware being ruined was feigned. In effect, it was a mockery of their orthodox Hindu ways and was most likely aimed at him. He did not know where her ideas came from, but he was revolted by the fuss she had created around that good-natured elderly gentleman. He suppressed that feeling and, with a little smile, told Bandana, 'Have you not heard from your didi that ours is a very orthodox Hindu home? Neither enamel nor porcelain goods are allowed here.'

'But so many expensive silver utensils will now have to be thrown away,' Bandana said.

Her father anxiously said, 'I have been told that if you heat them up after applying a spot of ghee, then...'

Bipradas paid no heed to it, but continued talking to Bandana, 'There is no shortage of silverware in this house. Your father is a revered elder and an honoured guest. We need to treat him honourably in keeping with his stature. If, for his visit, some silver utensils are thrown away, let it be so.' Then he smiled and said, 'If, like your didi, you are also married into an orthodox family, then you can serve your father in earthenware plates which you can throw away—and no harm will be done to anybody. What do you say to that, Bandana?'

'No way. For my father, I will get plates made of gold.'

Bipradas laughed and said, 'No, you won't. No one who would do so would speak about their father in the way you have done. Not even to put someone else down. I think there is someone who loves her uncle more than you love your father.'

On hearing that, Raysahib felt much relieved and his heart was filled with great happiness. He said, 'You are quite right. When my dada died, Sati was very small. Being employed abroad, it was not easy for me to come home often. Even when I did, the social taboo forced me to live by myself, but whenever Sati could, she would come and visit me.'

Bandana quickly intervened, 'Forget about it, Baba.'

'No, I remember—it is all true. Once she sat down to have a meal with me, and her mother was upset...'

'Baba,' Bandana protested, 'What is all this pointless talk? When did Mejdi sit down with you...? Your memory is adrift.'

'No, I remember it quite well. In case there should be any concerns about this, I should say that her mother was very perturbed.'

Bandana said, 'Baba, you will miss your train. Do you know what time it is?'

Concerned, Raysahib consulted his pocket watch and replied with relief, 'You scared me. There is enough time to catch the train.'

Bipradas laughed out loud and said, 'Yes, yes, there is time enough. Please relax and finish your meal. I will see you off at the station.' And then he left.

When Sati came in, Bandana spoke to her softly, 'Mejdi, did you hear what Father said?'

Sati said, 'Yes.'

'You will be in a spot of trouble if your mother-in-law hears this, won't you?'

'I could be if she comes to know of this, but let us not discuss it. Kaka may hear us.'

'But your husband heard everything. He will not overlook such a sin.'

'If I really did something wrong, why should I expect to be forgiven?' Sati said complacently. 'I will be quite content in leaving it to him to decide. You will see for yourself if you stay back. Kaka, what more can I give you?'

Raysahib looked up and said, 'Nothing more, please, nothing. I have had enough.'

It was time to proceed to the railway station. A car was waiting under the porch, with another car loaded with luggage. Raysahib was talking to Bipradas when, unexpectedly, Bandana appeared in her travel clothes. 'I am going with you, Baba,' she announced.

Raysahib was taken aback and asked, 'Why do you have to travel to the railway station in this hot sun?'

Bandana told him, 'I am not going just to the railway station, but to Calcutta. I can then return to Bombay with you.'

Bipradas was shocked. He said, 'How can this be? I believed you would be staying with us for a few days.'

Bandana just said, 'No.'

'But you have had nothing to eat.'

'Skipping a meal is no problem.'

'Does your mejdi know that you are leaving?'

Bandana replied, 'I really don't know, but she will when I am gone.'

Bipradas said, 'She will be very upset if you leave without eating anything.'

Bandana was unconcerned. She just said, 'But why? It is not that she invited me to stay and that all her arrangements will be ruined if I do not eat. She is no fool, she will understand.' Without speaking further, she climbed into the car.

It dawned on Raysahib that something must have gone wrong. His daughter was not the type to do anything precipitate. He said, 'It was also my impression that she would stay a few days with Sati. Now that she is already in the car, she is not going to come out.'

Bipradas said nothing and followed him into the car.

The car started moving. Looking up, Bandana saw Dwijadas standing at the open window of the library. When their eyes met, she folded her hands in greeting.

SEVEN

On reaching the railway station, they were told that their train would be late due to an accident somewhere—perhaps for an hour or more. The regular stationmaster having been taken ill, a South Indian substitute was in charge who had no idea how late the train would be.

Bipradas looked at Raysahib and said, 'It will be very late when you reach Calcutta. Must you go today?'

'Not really, I have...'

Bandana resisted, 'No, Baba, that will not do. Once you have left, you can't go back.'

Bipradas spoke almost pleadingly, 'But why not, Bandana? You came without eating anything, and this way you will go hungry the whole day.'

Somewhat aggrieved, Raysahib said, 'Their ways are different. Once they make up their minds, they find it difficult to change.'

Bipradas kept quiet.

Though it was not a major railway station, it did have a waiting room. On arriving, they found a young, anglicized

Bengali gentleman and his wife already installed there. The young man could have been a barrister or a doctor, or even a qualified English professor. It was a mystery as to what they were doing in that place. He rested on an easy chair, semi-inclined, with his two legs stretched out on the extended arms of the chair. When other people arrived, he just glanced at them through his half-shut eyes and did nothing else. The lady however stood up. Perhaps, she had not yet fully become a memsahib; though her high heels and her style of dress indicated that efforts were not lacking.

Locating another easy chair, Bandana led her father to it and then sat down on a bench. She very politely asked her brother-in-law not to keep standing but to sit near her. 'I believe that wood does not get tainted, so if you sit here, there will be no question of losing your caste,' she remarked.

Bandana's father smiled when he heard his daughter and asked, 'Is Bipradas very fussy about the issue of caste pollution?'

Bipradas also smiled and replied, 'Yes, it is an issue. But I cannot tell you how drastically, as I do not know the answer.'

'Taking, for instance, what Bandana said?'

Bipradas commented, 'She is angry as she had had no food. There is no point discussing anything that women say out of rage.'

Bandana said, 'No, I am not angry, not the slightest.'

Bipradas said, 'Yes, you are and very much so, or else you would have gone back to our home instead of going to Calcutta. Besides, you should have known that having travelled in the car together, I must have already lost my caste. Your point about losing my caste on sharing a bench with you is nothing but a mere pretence.'

Bandana said, 'That may be so, but please tell me honestly whether you will have to have another bath when you return home after being sullied by our touch.'

'Come back to our house. You can see whether I do or not with your eyes.'

'No. Do you know that when I went to touch your mother's feet, she retreated to avoid my touch?' Her face went red with resentment as she recounted her indignity.

Bipradas noticed that. He replied calmly, 'That is partly true, but not fully so. You will never know the real reason behind it unless you stay with us for some days. But that is clearly not possible.'

'No, it is not.'

The reason for Bandana's refusal was then clear to him and, because of it, he felt great remorse on many grounds. The remark about his stepmother was partially correct, but somehow also seemed to involve him. Yet, he had neither the time nor the opportunity to explain. On the other hand, Bandana showed no inclination to give him a patient hearing or to appreciate what he had to say. Bipradas had no alternative but to keep quiet, and that was what he did.

The young, anglicized gentleman put his feet down and, after a yawn, asked, 'Are you not Bipradasbabu, the zamindar?'

'Yes.'

'I have heard of you. My wife's maternal uncle's home is in the next village and, since we came to Bengal, she has been very keen to meet him. That is what brings us here. I have my practice in Punjab.'

Bipradas looked at him and estimated that he was more or less his age—perhaps a few years either way.

The young man continued, 'We were just talking about you yesterday. People say you are a terrible, I mean, a very tough zamindar. A few Brahmins there also lauded you as a conservative Hindu. I now find this to be true.'

Those uncalled for remarks from a stranger confounded both the father and the daughter, but Bipradas did not react. It was likely that he was so distracted that he might not have heard him.

The gentleman went on, 'In my lectures, I often say that there is no place in education for tricks and hoaxes; education must be rock solid. You ought to visit Europe at least once. If you do not absorb the atmosphere of that country and breathe their free air, you will not experience mental freedom. You will never be rid of superstitions. I lived there for five years.'

The last few words pleased Bandana's father enormously. He concurred, 'Yes, very true.'

Given that pat on the back, the young gentleman continued more excitedly, 'In this day of modern democracy, all are equal and no one is inferior to anyone. Each person must assert their own rights, regardless of consequences. Had I had that kind of money, I would have arranged for all your tenants to visit Europe so that they could learn their rights.'

Bandana could not take that sort of talk lying down. She said in a muffled voice, 'Whoever gave you the impression that my brother-in-law tyrannizes his tenants? Was your in-laws' family subjected to some hardship?'

'Ah, this gentleman is your brother-in-law, is he?' the young man responded. 'No, we do not have a complaint against him.' He turned to his wife and said, 'I wish your sisters were like her. Perhaps, you have already been to Europe? No? Then you must go and see for yourself the women there—their freedom, courage, and strength. On my next visit, I will take my wife with me.'

Soon thereafter, the substitute stationmaster came in and told them that their train was about to arrive, at which all of them rushed to the platform. The train was packed; there was no room at all. It was filled with a holiday crowd. There was only a single first-class carriage and a single second class, and the second class was filled with Anglo-Indian railway employees travelling to Calcutta on the occasion of some sporting event. A few of them spilled over into the first-class carriage. Drunk with an excess of alcohol, they looked terrible. Blocking the door of the carriage, they shouted, 'There is no room, go away, go away!'

The young gentleman said, 'So, what now?'

Bandana was alarmed and suggested, 'Let us go back home.'

'No,' Bipradas said firmly.

'Why not? We can take the night train.'

The young gentleman agreed, 'What else can we do?'

Bipradas disapproved, 'There are only four or five men in the chamber, and there is ample room for another four or five.'

Bandana's father added nervously, 'But they are all dead drunk.'

With steely resolve, Bipradas said, 'That is their pleasure, not our fault. Get into the carriage. I will come with you.' He forced open the door, pulled Bandana by the hand, and asked her to go in. To the young gentleman, he said, 'If you wish to assert your rights, go in with your wife. With the tyrannical zamindar with you, you should have no problem.'

The drunken Anglo-Indian lot, having taken a look at Bipradas, shifted to one corner of the coach.

EIGHT

Some of their fellow travellers in the other carriage came down to help their friends in order to show off their power.

Bipradas summoned the guard and told him, 'I do not think these men are first-class passengers. It is your duty to take them away.'

The guard was also a sahib, but a pretty dark one. Regardless of his duty, he appeared hesitant. Bipradas beckoned to the substitute stationmaster and, giving him a five-rupee note, told him, 'My servants will give you my name. Send a wire to your higher authorities in my name informing them that a group of drunken Anglo-Indians was unlawfully occupying a first-class compartment and were refusing to vacate. Also tell them that the guard was watching it all, but did not lift a finger to help.'

The guard realized that he was in a fix. Picking up courage, he told the Anglo-Indians, 'Can't you see they are important people? You are all railway employees travelling on the railway pass, so be careful.'

Though drunk, they dared not ignore that caution. So they vacated the compartment, but not before muttering some threats. The young sahib profusely thanked the guard, telling him that but for him they might not have been able to travel.

'Oh no, Sir. It is my duty.'

The bell rang for the train to leave. Bipradas said, 'There is no need for me to go. They will not create any more trouble.'

The young barrister confirmed, 'They will not dare. The fear of loss of their jobs will deter them.'

Bandana barred the door. 'No, you can't. Job security is not the only security—you have to come with us.'

Bipradas laughed, 'Had you been a man, you would have appreciated that there is no greater guarantee in life than that. Anyway, I had nothing to eat before I left.'

'Neither had I.'

'That was your choice. Soon enough, you will reach a major station with many food outlets, and if you so wish, you can have something to eat there.'

'I have no such desire,' Bandana said, 'I can keep a fast as well.'

'That helps no one. Allow me to leave now.' Looking at the barrister sahib, he said, 'Please keep an eye on them. If needed...'

'Pull the emergency chain to stop the train,' Bandana interrupted, 'I am quite capable of doing it.' She put her head out and told the servants, 'Tell Mother that he is accompanying us. He will return tomorrow or the day after.'

The train left. Bandana spoke to Bipradas, 'You are very stubborn, are you not?'

'Why do you say that?'

'You forced us into the coach when the drunken lot was still there. What if they had not gone out and instead created trouble for us?'

'In that case, they would have lost their jobs,' Bipradas answered coolly.

'What about us? What if our bones were broken? Surely, that is no less serious than their loss of jobs?'

Both Bandana and Bipradas laughed, and the other lady also smiled, but the young barrister from Punjab turned solemn.

Bandana's father had not been paying any attention to what was happening, but catching the drift of their talk, he sat up straight and said, 'No, it is not a matter of joke. This is almost a regular feature of railway journeys that often get reported in the newspapers. I was not too keen in forcing our way—we could have easily taken the night train.'

'But what if there were drunks in the night train also?' Bandana asked.

Her father said, 'That would be unlikely. If that were the case, how could decent people ever travel by rail?'

Bandana spoke to Bipradas in a lowered voice, 'Please don't get into an argument with Father on the definition of decent people.'

Bipradas smiled and shook his head, 'Yes, I follow you.'

'Mukhujyemashai, did you ever get into a fight with Europeans in the maidan when you were a boy?'

'No, I have had no such luck.'

'I understand that you are a terror to your people. I believe that everyone is scared of you as though you are a tiger. Is it true?'

'Who has told you this?'

Bandana answered in a muted voice, 'Mejdi. She says that fear turns their blood into water.'

'Well, it is necessary,' Bipradas responded, 'or else we cannot keep women under control. When you get married, I will go and tutor your husband.'

Bandana said, 'Fine, do so, but remember that lessons do not necessarily work. I am sure you know this. Mejdi is a good-natured person, but if it were me, I would be the one people would be scared of.'

'Meaning that fear of you would turn everybody's blood to water? I am not surprised given what I saw today of your conduct. Mother certainly is unlikely to forget this ever.'

Bandana agitatedly said, 'Do you know what your mother did? She stepped back when I went to touch her feet.'

Bipradas was not surprised. He just said, 'That is all you saw of Mother, nothing else. If you had, you would not have made the mistake of leaving without eating.'

'But surely there is something known as self-respect.'

Bipradas smiled and said, 'And where did you find this concept of self-respect? By reading fat treatises in your school and college, is that not so? But Mother knows no English, nor has she read any books, so how can she have ideas like you?'

'Even so, I can carry on with my ideas,' Bandana retaliated.

Bipradas replied, 'That can lead to committing faux pas, as you did today. You could do it only because you are so deeply engrossed in the lessons learnt from foreign books. Otherwise, you would have hesitated to show such disrespect to a senior relative. You would have appreciated the distinction between dignity and vanity.'

Whether Bandana appreciated the distinction or not, she realized that her conduct that day had hurt Bipradas, not for himself, but because of the disrespect to his mother.

'Are you also an orthodox Hindu like your mother?' asked Bandana.

'I am, yes,' Bipradas confirmed.

'And do you believe in the issue of caste pollution?'

'I do.'

'So if I try to touch your feet, you will move away.'

'I may, depending on the circumstances.'

'I presume that Mejdi has been converted to a blind follower as well?'

'She too has to observe the family customs.'

'Meaning that no one can disobey the tiger.'

Bipradas smiled.

Bandana carried on, 'Mejdi is a woman, and so naturally a weak person. It was easy to force family customs on her, but I believe Dijubabu does not comply with the family law, so what does Mr Tiger say to that?'

Bandana's question was intended as a barb, which Bipradas ignored. Smiling as before, he said, 'Personal issues cannot be discussed in the absence of the individual concerned.'

'Will Dijubabu ever know where he stands?'

'In time, yes. He does know that tigers are not choosy about their victims.'

Bandana turned pale and said nothing. The change did not escape Bipradas's sharp eyes. She was afraid to raise the topic of Dwijadas, so she said, 'I am not too worried about Mejdi's mother-in-law, but I shall be awfully sorry if Mejdi feels hurt because I left without eating. That thought is nagging me.'

Bipradas said tersely, 'The issue of your mejdi's unhappiness takes precedence in your mind over my mother's pain; her feeling of embarassment counts for nothing. When a person has no clue as to the reality, one's thoughts go awry.'

Bandana shot back, 'How do you mean awry? It is only but natural.'

Bipradas remained silent, and Bandana realized that he was displeased.

It was getting dark. Nothing was visible outside, yet Bandana kept looking out of the window. The train should have reached Howrah station by then, but it was going to be late that evening by about two hours. Bandana turned to see Bipradas writing in a notebook. She said, 'Mukhujyemashai, may I ask you something?'

'Yes, what?'

'You hinted that my concept of dignity is just borrowed from schoolbooks, but your mother did not go to any school. What then is the source of her dignity?'

Caught off guard, Bipradas kept quiet.

Bandana continued, 'Somehow, my curiosity about her haunts me. I admit that she is a senior kinsperson, but is that the most important issue in life above everything else?'

There was no response from Bipradas.

'Yes, I agree that we were uninvited guests in her home, but does that justify overlooking my dignity because I am younger in age?'

Bipradas still remained quiet.

Bandana went on, 'Nevertheless, I ask for her forgiveness, and I do trust that my conduct will not cause any distress to Mejdi. My mother had travelled to England with my father, which, your mother believes, had turned my mother into a memsahib. Because of this belief, apparently, there is no end to the abusive treatment meted out to Mejdi. Your mother's beliefs and mine will never match; still, a slight is a slight, even though it comes from a senior person like your mother.' Her eyes filled with tears as she said this.

Bipradas said softly, 'My mother did not insult you.'

'Of course, she did,' Bandana insisted.

Bipradas paused for a while before replying, 'No, my mother did not insult you; but only she can explain this to you. In order to understand her actions, one has to be with her. Arguing on this won't help.'

Bandana turned her face to look out of the window.

Bipradas continued, 'Once my parents had a disagreement over a trifling issue, which later snowballed into a quarrel. While I cannot tell you everything, I can only say that on that day, I appreciated how deep-rooted was the sense of dignity of my uneducated mother.'

Bandana turned round and observed how his intense pride in his mother had lit up his face.

Bipradas went on, 'Sometime after this, I asked Mother what the source of her great dignity was.'

'And what did she say?' asked Bandana.

Bipradas answered, 'Perhaps, you know that she is really not my mother. She has two children of her own—Diju and

Kalyani. She told me that the person who put her in charge of bringing up the three children together was the very person who instilled this in her. Since then, because of her sense of deep dignity, no one ever realized that she was not my mother, but my stepmother. Do you appreciate the significance of this?'

After a pause, he resumed, 'Some people have a heightened sense of self-respect, taking offence at minor deviations—how did one react to someone's greeting; how low did one bow one's head while greeting someone with folded hands; and so on and so forth. You will find examples galore of such clashes of ego in every country, and plenty of stories of obsession with pride litter the pages of your schoolbooks. But the day my mother, even before she herself was a mother, entered this large family, assuming motherhood of someone else's child, many relatives who had found their home here became vituperative. But Mother converted them all not by enforcing her authority as the lady of the house, but through her own dignity. And that was so supreme that no one could ever cross it.'

Overwhelmed by his words, Bandana stared at Bipradas.

Suddenly, the barrister sahib exclaimed, 'The train has finally reached Howrah station!'

Bandana's father was probably dozing. He woke up and said, 'Ah, that's a relief.'

Bandana spoke in a subdued voice, 'I don't feel like going to Calcutta, Mukhujyemashai. I would rather go back to your mother and tell her that I was wrong and ask her to forgive me.'

Bipradas smiled and said nothing.

At the station, Bipradas asked, 'Where are you all staying?'

Bandana's father said, 'We normally stay at the Grand Hotel, and that is where we shall go. I have already made a reservation.'

The talk about Grand Hotel in Bipradas's presence made Bandana uncomfortable.

The young barrister from Punjab continued to curse the railways for being so late and kept complaining that he would be forced to spend the night in the railway waiting room, as he had to catch his connecting train from there.

Bipradas was waiting. Bandana's father suggested, 'Bipradas, why do you not also come with us to the Grand Hotel?'

'Grand Hotel?' Bipradas was amused. 'Please do not worry about me. Diju has a home at Bowbazar, well-furnished and with a complement of servants. I come to Calcutta often and stay there. Why do you not all come there with me?'

Bandana was thrilled. 'Yes, a great idea. We shall all go there.' She felt immensely relieved and, in her exultation, extended an invitation to the barrister couple.

NINE

When Bandana got up in the morning, she discovered that her conjecture about the house was entirely wrong. She had assumed that a rented home of a man—and that too a bachelor—would be untended, with accumulated dirt at the corners, stains of spit and betel juice, broken-down furniture, dirty beds, soot clinging to beams and joists, and cobwebs everywhere. She had not had a good look in the dim light of the previous night, but she was impressed that morning by the neatness and tidiness everywhere. It was a big house with many rooms and balconies—all bright and clean. Outside her room, Bandana met a middle-aged widow who looked as if she were from a modest background. To Bandana's great discomfort, she touched her feet.

She told Bandana, 'I have been waiting for you. I am a maidservant here. Let me show you the bathroom.'

'Is my father awake?' asked Bandana.

'He went to bed late, so it is likely that he would be up late.'

'And the other couple who came with us?'

'They are still in bed.'

'And your barababu? Is he also in bed?'

The maidservant smiled, 'No. He already had his dip in the Ganges, completed his puja, and is now in the office room. Shall I send him a message?'

Bandana said, 'No, that isn't necessary.'

The bathroom was located a little further away across a small verandah. On the way, Bandana asked, 'I suppose that in this home, a bathroom cannot be close to the bedrooms.'

The maidservant replied, 'No, that is not possible, as Ma is frequently here when she comes to visit the Kali temple.'

Bandana pondered. The mother's all-powerful writ, bound by rigorous religious rites and regulations, ran even here. She went back to her room to collect her clothes and asked the maidservant, 'We may need to be here for a few more days, so what shall I call you? Are there any other maidservants?'

She replied, 'There is another, but she has a great deal to do and cannot find the time to come upstairs. But whatever you need, Didi, do ask me. My name is Annada. But since I am from a village, I may make mistakes.'

Her humility pleased Bandana. She asked, 'Where is your home? Who else is there?'

Annada said, 'Our home is Balarampur—the same place as my employers. I have a son. The babus educated him and gave him a job. He lives in the village with his wife. He is fine, Didi.'

'In that case, why do you still work for a living?' Bandana was curious. 'Why do you not stay at home with your son and daughter-in-law?'

Annada said, 'I would love to, Didi, but can't. In my difficult times, I gave my word to the babus that if my son grows up to be successful, I will take charge of looking after other people's sons. I cannot shake off that responsibility. Many boys from our village study in Calcutta. Other than me, there is no one else to take care of them.'

'Do these boys live in this house?'

'Yes, they do, and they go to college. But you are getting late. I will wait outside. Just call me when you need me.'

On entering the bathroom, Bandana found that it had many fixtures and conveniences. There were three rooms beside it, all with arrangements in place to avoid pollution by touch. All of that had clearly been done keeping Mother in mind. The marble floor, a marble stool, three large copper vessels, presumably for storing Ganges water, were all spotlessly shining. No one knew when she was there last or when her next visit would be, yet all was kept meticulous and spotless as though she were a permanent resident here. There were no signs of any neglect. It took no time for Bandana to appreciate that the orderly state of affairs was not achieved just by fiat; a far stronger force was regulating all that. The mother, a singular lady, who was held so high above everybody, occupied Bandana's thought for a considerable time. She had, of course, read in many books about the repression and the ignominious condition of Indian women and, being a woman, that plight of Indian women made her ashamed. These reports were not unjust, and yet, standing in that bathroom all by herself, they did not appear to be wholly true.

As she came out of the bathroom, Annada told her, 'It is very late, Didi. They are all waiting for you in the dining room. Please, let us go.'

'Has your barababu come out of office?'

'Yes, he is down there as well.'

'I suspect he will not eat with us.'

Annada answered with a smile, 'Even if he eats, that will only be in the afternoon. And today, he won't even take that. Being ekadashi, he will just eat some fruits in the evening.'

Bandana felt that the woman was not just a maidservant in this house. 'He is not a widow in a Brahmin family, so what makes him observe the ekadashi fast? Last night, he did not exactly have his ekadashi fast. Instead, he had a dashami fast.'

Annada said, 'It does not matter really. Fasting does not bother him. Ma says that in his previous birth, Bipin had received a boon through his penances to be fast-proof in this birth. The restraint in his eating habits is truly astounding.'

Down in the dining room, Bandana found that their customary breakfast of tea, bread, and eggs were all neatly arranged on the table, and her father, the barrister from Punjab, and his wife were impatient with hunger. Almost at the end of his patience, Raysahib, discarding the newspaper that he was reading, said in a petulant voice, 'You are so late! How will we get any work done this morning!'

Finding Bipradas there, Bandana asked, 'Are you not having anything to eat, Mukhujyemashai?'

Bipradas took the hint. He smiled and said, 'I don't drink tea. All that I have is plain rice and dal. This is not the time for it, so do not worry about me. Sit down and have your breakfast.'

Bandana apologized to her father and the other two guests, 'Sorry, it is my fault. I should have sent a message earlier, but did not manage to do so. I do not feel like eating. Do not wait for me. Start your breakfast. I will pour the tea.'

Everyone was concerned. Raysahib asked anxiously, 'Are you unwell?'

'No, Father, I am fine. I just don't feel like eating.'

'In that case, don't. Perhaps, the late dinner last night did not agree with you.'

'That is possible. Later, I will have some rice and dal along with Mukhujyemashai. I am sure I can digest that in this house.'

Nobody else paid any heed to it, but a shadow crossed Bipradas's mind.

A servant who was there blurted out, 'It is ekadashi today. He will have only some fruits in the evening and nothing else.'

Bandana already knew this, yet, feigning surprise, she said, 'Just some fruits? A light meal. It will be great, will it not, Mukhujyemashai?'

Bipradas nodded, but the fact that someone could so easily make fun of him annoyed him. Bandana glanced at him and understood that.

It was late in the afternoon when Bandana and her father returned after completing their chores. Barrister sahib and his wife were out sightseeing. They were supposed to have travelled by the night train, but had apparently deferred their journey.

Raysahib went up to his room to change. Bandana met Annada outside her room. She laughingly complained to Bandana, 'Didi, you have had nothing to eat the whole day. I have brought fruits for you. Now go and have a wash while I get everything ready for you.'

'Your barababu—where is he?'

'He has gone to Dakhshineshwar, the Kali temple. He should be back soon.'

'Fine. I will eat when he returns. But what is being prepared for the rest of the guests? Come, let me have a look at your kitchen.'

'If you so wish, but their food for the evening is not being cooked in the kitchen. The food will come from a hotel.'

Bandana was shocked. 'What? Whoever suggested this?'

'Barababu himself.'

'But where will they consume all this prohibited food? In this house? What will your ma say if she comes to know about this?'

Annada said, 'No, she will not come to know about this. All arrangements are being made in a ground-floor room. The necessary pots, pans, plates, and other things will be supplied by the hotel, so there should be no problem.'

'Well, Barababu ordered all this, but who carried out the order? Can you take me to him?'

'Certainly, Didi. Please come with me.'

The family had a large moneylending operation in Calcutta. The ground floor housed an office to conduct the business, consisting of four rooms in which the required staff worked. The employees all stood up as Bandana entered. Correctly identifying the manager, she beckoned him to come out of the room and asked him, 'Was it you who ordered the food from the hotel?'

When the manager nodded yes, Bandana instructed him to go back to the hotel and cancel the order.

Confused, the manager said hesitatingly, 'But, until Barababu returns...'

Bandana countered, 'It may be too late to cancel then. If Barababu gets angry, he will be angry with me. You have nothing to be afraid of. Please go, don't waste time.'

'What a mess,' thought the manager, dumbfounded. It was difficult to disobey Bipradas, almost impossible, but it was no less difficult to ignore the positive and the firm counter instructions of this unknown young lady—almost equally impossible. He stood there undecided and then said irresolutely, 'Well, as you say. Let me go and cancel the order. Some advance money has been paid.'

'It doesn't matter. Please go. Do not delay,' said Bandana.

Upon his return that evening, Bipradas heard all of it. He was in two minds whether to be pleased or displeased. He discovered that almost everything was ready in the kitchen, and Bandana, sitting on a stool, was busy dealing with the cook. She stood up and asked in mock modesty, 'I trust, Mukhujyemashai, that you have not sacked your manager in anger?'

Bipradas asked, 'Who told you that Mukhujyemashai was such an ill-tempered person?'

Bandana said, 'Do you not know that a tiger can be smelled from miles away?'

Bipradas laughed. 'But what about the guests? They are all used to western-style dinner—so what about that?'

'Please pack those who cannot do without a western-style meal off to a hotel. I will pay for it. What an unpleasant thing it would be if all that food was brought into this house! What would Ma's reaction be when she heard about it?'

Not that it had not occurred to Bipradas, but he could not make up his mind. He just said, 'No way would she come to know about this.'

Bandana shook her head. 'Yes, she would. I would have written to her.'

'Why?'

'Why? Why would you do something simply for some odd, temporary guests that you have never done before? No, never.'

Bandana's reply not only pleased Bipradas immensely, but it also astounded him. After a pause, he said, 'But Bandana, you have had nothing to eat since yesterday. Are you still angry with me?' His voice had a touch of affection.

Bandana replied softly, 'But why did you make me angry? Anyway, please listen to me. Fruits have been acquired for your consumption. Please go and perform your evening puja, meanwhile I will get everything ready. If someone else, and not me, fetches your food, I will not eat at all today.'

'Alright, do that,' said Bipradas and went up.

About an hour later, Bandana returned, bearing a white marble plate containing fruits and sweets. Annada followed with a cushion and drinking water. Bandana made a place ready for him to eat, cleansing it carefully with water.

Looking at Bandana, Bipradas spoke with a degree of surprise, 'But why did you have a bath now?'

Bandana put the plate down and said, 'Please sit down and eat.'

TEN

Having taken his seat, Bipradas asked the same question, 'Did you really have to have a bath again now? You may catch a cold.'

'I may, but it is my intention not to let you have an excuse to refuse taking food touched by me. You will have to declare clearly that I am an outcaste and so you cannot eat food served by me.'

Bipradas laughed and said, 'Have you not read in your books that an evil person does not lack in excuses?'

'I have indeed, but to me you are neither an evil person nor a terror. You are a normal human being like us—a mixture of virtue and vices. Otherwise, I would not have cancelled your dinner plans for the other guests.'

'Can you tell me the truth?'

'I have already told you. This is not normal in your family, neither in your village home nor here. Then why should you do this now?'

'But do you not know that they have all lived in England and are used to western-style food?'

'Regardless of what they are used to, they are still Bengali, and I have never known any instance when a Bengali guest has died on being denied western food. Ergo, your pretext is utterly pointless.'

Bipradas asked, 'What then, according to you, will not be pointless?'

Bandana said, 'Frankly, I don't really know. But I feel that what you say publicly, you do not wholly believe. Or else, you would not have agreed to do this arrangement behind your mother's back. People are not all that scared of you, as generally believed. It is not you, but your mother whom they fear the most.'

Bipradas did not appear to be annoyed. On the contrary, he smiled and said, 'Yes, you have summed up both of us well. But who told you that the plan was being made behind my mother's back?'

Bandana named no one and said, 'That I found out through my enquiries. But this was going to be such a major disaster that my mejdi would have never forgiven me. She would be cursing me forever, thinking that I was at the root of this calamity. That is why I could not have allowed you to go ahead with this plan.'

Bipradas said, 'You are a close relative, and so what you did was quite appropriate. But did you also find out if I could clandestinely eat food served by you? If not, then go back and find out while I wait for your answer.' He smiled and pushed away his plate.

Bandana went red with embarassment, but, having composed herself, she retorted, 'No, I am not inclined to check this out, and if that means you will not eat, so be it.'

'But the problem is,' said Bipradas, 'I really cannot keep you unfed in my house.' And he resumed eating.

Bandana asked, 'What happens after this?'

'I just have to go home and do some penance, which may include consuming cow dung.' Saying so, he laughed. Despite that, Bandana was not sure if it was a joke or the truth. She turned pensive.

Bipradas continued, 'I will have to come to an understanding with Mother. More importantly, I will be reprieved from your sister's reprimand.' He paused and resumed with a smile, 'So you don't believe me? Well, you will appreciate this truth after you get married.' He finished eating and got up.

The dinner order might have been cancelled, but there was no shortage of tasty dishes in the house. The guests were all replete. At the end of the day, Bandana lay in her bed deep in thought. Bipradas's attitude towards her was not unexpected, perhaps not even unfair. It was also pointless to bring up the issue, for, though closely related, they had not known each other for any length of time and, on that pretext, to hurt him would be merely churlish. To avoid being sullied by her touch, Bipradas's mother had stepped away when Bandana went to touch her feet. Bandana, stung, had come away in protest from their house without any food. It was not that the aggressive religious belief of an unlettered woman did not hurt, though it was possible some day to overlook that misguided action, but Bandana had no clue how to take exception to what Bipradas did. True, he did eat the food served by her, not willingly, but out of obligation, just to avoid a repetition of the unsavoury incident at Balarampur. Her disregard of convention did bother Bipradas, but the very thought that he had to do a penance back home continued to haunt Bandana and robbed her of sleep. Why should that incident snowball into such a severe affair? Their paths in life were not the same, but there should be space enough for either of them. How did it matter if there was a conflict? And why did the issue continue to plague her? She tried to calm herself, but she could not rid her mind of his silent disregard of her.

Sleep did eventually overtake her, but not for long. It was not yet dawn when she woke up and, though sleepy, she left her bed and went out to the verandah. Leaning against the railing, she observed that the sky was still dark and, save for the occasional sound of traffic from the main road, the house was absolutely quiet. She found Mother's puja room lit up; perhaps the servants had forgotten to turn down the lamps, or was it that Bipradas had sat down for his puja?

Bandana became intensely curious. It would be most embarrassing if he spotted her, because there could hardly be an excuse for her to be there at this time of the night. But she could not contain her curiosity.

Bandana knew about meditation from her reading, and had also seen pictures, but had never witnessed it. In the lonely darkness of the silent night, she came across that sight. With both his eyes closed, the tall and strong body of Bipradas sat motionless, the light from above reflecting on his face and body. Perhaps, it was nothing special. Had she seen it another time, Bandana might have been amused, but through her still drowsy eyes, what she saw then mesmerized her. She lost count of how long she stood there watching, but when she came to her senses, she noticed that the eastern sky was streaked with light. It was about time for the servants to get up. She waited no longer; returning to her room, she promptly fell into a deep sleep.

Annada woke her up by knocking on the door. 'Didi, it is very late, are you not getting up?'

Bandana hurriedly came out and saw that she was indeed very late. She asked diffidently, 'I suppose the other guests are waiting for me this morning as well? Why did you not wake me up earlier? I don't think I can be ready within an hour.'

Looking at her troubled face, Annada smiled and assured her, 'Don't worry, Didi. The other guests did not wait today— they had had their food already. So take your time at bath—no one is going to bother you.'

'Don't you ever feel hungry in the morning?' asked Annada.

'Never, though we always had breakfast as a child. But let me not waste any more time,' saying so, Bandana pushed off.

A couple of hours later, she met Bipradas downstairs. He was coming out from his office. Bandana greeted him.

'Have you had your breakfast?' asked Bipradas.

'Yes.'

'The others could not wait, but you...'

Bandana stopped him, 'But I have no grouse on that score, Mukhujyemashai.'

Bipradas smiled and said, 'Your temperament is praiseworthy. That I will not deny. You two sisters are poles apart—like the sun and the moon. I believe you will soon travel to England to complete your education. Let me know when you come back. I will go and see you in your new manifestation.'

Bandana smiled, but did not react.

Bipradas teased her, 'I believe that the people in that country remain in bed till midday; a rather difficult task. You may not have much of a problem. After all, you already are used to it.'

Bandana smiled again and said nothing, but kept looking at Bipradas. He looked a normal, decent person. He was one of those affectionate souls who always joked and smiled. But the image of him from that morning, sitting motionless, deep in meditation, seemed so mystifying that her curiosity continued unabated.

'But where are the others? I don't see anyone,' Bandana said.

Bipradas said, 'That means they are not here. Your father and the barrister couple—all three—have gone to Howrah station to book their berths.'

Bandana wondered, 'I can understand the barrister couple doing that, but why my father? He has still eight or ten days of leave. And that too without telling me.'

Bipradas said, 'Perhaps, he did not get the time to tell you. I understand that he received an urgent telegram from his office. I inferred from his look that he may have to return earlier.'

'But why should I have to go back so soon? I can't.'

'That is my view also. Why must you go?'

Not quite following him, Bandana looked at him quizzically.

Bipradas answered her, 'I suggest that you send a telegram to your sister, asking her to come along with her brother-in-law. It will suit both of you, and I will be relieved of looking after the guests.'

'But how can that be?' Bandana asked anxiously. 'Will your mother agree to this? She cannot stand me.'

Bipradas replied, 'Why not give it a try? Shall I get you a telegraph form?'

She looked expectantly at him and said, 'No, Mukhujyemashai, I cannot do this.'

'So be it then.'

'Better that I return with Father.'

'If you so wish.'

Bandana picked up the telegram that her father had received. It was indeed from his office. The situation was urgent, so there was no way in which he could defer his return.

Bandana went back to her room and commenced packing. Her father had still not returned when Annada handed her a telegram that had arrived for her. Much perplexed, she found that the telegram was from Dayamoyee asking her not to go back with her father and also telling her that her didi would be travelling to Calcutta by that night's train along with Diju.

ELEVEN

The news of her didi's arrival along with Dwijadas pleased her
to no end. She was very ashamed of her conduct at her didi's
home, yet she could not find a way to make amends for it.
Despite her unwillingness, she was going to return to Bombay
with her father; but, unexpectedly, her crisis had been resolved.
She eagerly waited for her father to return to show him the
telegram. She discovered that Bipradas had gone out. Truthfully,
there was no need to tell him because, as she suspected, he
must have been at the root of that development. At first, she
had not taken to this hard and conservative scion of the much
maligned zamindar class. Though he still remained inscrutable,
there was now a slow change in her outlook. She found that
he was a man of few words, his attitude was moderate, and
his manners congenial and gentle, yet an air of aloofness was
evident in each of his moves. Though living in a close-knit
family, he seemed to be separate from all of them. Sheltered
poor relations, servants (men or women), and office workers—
all of them respected him and were devoted to him, but they
also feared him. Their thoughts about him were somewhat

like—Barababu was the provider of their bread. He was their protector, their support during difficult times, but he was not close to anyone. At the time of one's father's death, one could speak to him of one's bereavement and obligations, but one couldn't invite him to eat with them on the occasion of the marriage of one's son. One could not conceive of such familiarity.

Finding the kitchen maid last night rather naïve, she probed her to get to the bottom of this fear complex of Barababu. But despite incisive cross-examination, all that she could extract from her was that she too was as scared as everyone else. Perhaps, others would have echoed the same feeling. While travelling with Bipradas the other day in the train, the evidence of his strong character had surfaced briefly, but had retreated quickly. Their pleasant light-hearted talks during the journey gave her no clue that the same man was the barababu of that home.

Suddenly, she heard sounds coming from downstairs. Someone came running to tell her that her father had returned from the station, but with a foot injury. Looking through a window, she saw that the barrister from Punjab and his wife were helping Raysahib get out of the car. He was without a shoe and sock on one foot, which was wrapped with wet handkerchiefs. In the rush of the station platform, someone had dropped a heavy wooden box on his foot. Raysahib was taken to his room, and a doctor was sent for. The doctor bandaged his foot, prescribed medicines, and advised the patient to avoid walking for a few days.

The next afternoon, Sati arrived and Bandana joyfully went to welcome her, but all her pleasure was dampened when she found that along with her mejdi had also arrived her mother-in-law, Dayamoyee. Bandana stiffly touched her feet and was about to move away when Dayamoyee touched her chin and kissed her. She asked her pleasantly, 'Are you all right, child?'

Bandana nodded her head, 'Yes, I am. But, Ma, what brings you here so unexpectedly?'

'What else could I have done?' Dayamoyee said. 'A tetchy child of mine left in anger without eating, and unless I can take her back after pacifying her, my child, how can I have any peace of mind?'

Bandana said with a diffident smile, 'But what makes you think that I came away because I was angry?'

'You have to wait till you have your own children. When you raise them and see them grow up, as I have done, only then you will know how mothers know when a daughter is irritated.' She said this ever so sweetly that Bandana once again bowed down and touched her feet and then said, 'Ma, my father is very unwell.'

'Unwell? What is wrong with him?'

She told Ma what had happened. 'He hurt his feet and has been in bed since yesterday. He cannot stand on his feet.'

Dayamoyee was very concerned. 'I trust that he has had proper medical care. Take me to your father's room. He is clearly the priority now above anything else.' Taking Sati with her, she followed Bandana to Raysahib's room. His pain had abated somewhat by then, so he sat up on the bed and greeted his visitor with folded arms. Dayamoyee reciprocated his greeting and asked, 'I say, Beimashai, how did you break your leg? What were you trying to get into?'

Sati and Bandana hid their smiles at the jest, and poor Raysahib, an innocent soul, protested that he had not tried to get into anything, and that the accident had happened at the open platform through no fault of his.

Dayamoyee smiled and said, 'Well, what has happened has happened. So stay here for some more days in the care of your daughters. Since one daughter may not be able to keep a check on you, I brought another daughter. Let the two of them take care of you by turn.'

Raysahib believed that to be the truth and offered many grateful thanks to Dayamoyee for showing such great compassion and sympathy.

'We will meet again. Now let me go and have a wash,' Dayamoyee said, and then left.

A second car brought Dwijadas and his nephew, Basudeb. Bandana had not met her mejdi's son that day at Balarampur, as he was away in school. Basudeb could not stay away from his grandmother, so he came with her and would go back with her.

After his uncle introduced them, Basudeb touched Bandana's feet. He was amazed by the shoes on Bandana's feet, but said nothing.

Bandana drew him close to her and asked, 'Do you not recognize me, Basu?'

'Yes, I do, Mashima.'

'But how could you have? You were no more than five years old when we met last. It is unlikely for you to remember.'

'I do, Mashima. I recognized you the day when you arrived, but did not see you when I returned from school because, by then, you had left our home as you were cross with us.'

'And who told you that I had left because I was cross?'

'I heard Kakababu telling Thakurma.'

Dwijadas chipped in, 'Not just me, everyone knows about it. At any rate, you did not make any effort to keep it under wraps.'

Bandana said, 'I see. So everyone knows that I was angry, but do they know why?'

Dwijadas said, 'Others may not, but I do. It was because Raysahib was asked to eat all by himself at a separate table.'

'In that case, do you think I was undeservedly disturbed?'

Dwijadas said, 'No, I don't, but others in our house would.'

'But you could have joined my father and eaten with him.'

'Yes, I could have, but not if Dada had asked me not to.'

'No? But what authority has your Dada to stop you?'

Dwijadas replied, 'That is Dada's business, not mine. All I know is that it would be wrong of me to defy him.'

Bandana asked, 'Tell me, do you not even dare to do what you regard as your duty?'

Dwijadas reflected for a while. 'This is not exactly a matter of daring or cowardice. By nature, I am not a timid person. But I cannot conceive of defying any specific prohibition of Dada's. As a young man, I had defied my father a number of times. Not that I went unpunished, but Dada is a person of a different disposition. Nobody can ignore him—ever.'

'And what happens if someone does?'

'Frankly, I do not know the answer. But this has never been an issue in our family.'

Bandana said, 'I know from Mejdi's letter that you do a great deal for the country, but against your Dada's wishes. How do you do that?'

Dwijadas replied, 'Yes, I do that against his will, but not against his specific injunction. That I could not have done.'

'Apparently, the impression I had formed of you from Didi's letters is not correct,' Bandana observed. 'I can now assure Didi that she has no cause for alarm. In your drama of serving the country, the huge property of Mukhujye family will not lose even a penny. Didi can be rest assured.'

Dwijadas smiled, 'Surely, you do not wish your didi to suffer a loss?'

A vexed Bandana said, 'What nonsense! Why should I wish that? All I wish is that they should be free of anxiety.'

'Have no worry,' said Dwijadas, 'they are free of any sense of threat. I can assert unhesitatingly that Dada does not know what fear is. That is against his nature.'

Bandana laughed, 'That means that the stock of fear has been distributed between all the members of the family except him, right?'

'Yes, something of that sort, but you will also not go without your share of whatever little remains of that. Have you still not got to know him despite being with him for three or four days?'

Shaking her head, Bandana said, 'Not really, but I am hoping to do that through you.'

'In that case, this is your first lesson. Please take your shoes off.'

A servant came and informed that Ma wanted them upstairs.

On the way up, Bandana asked, 'What brings Ma here?'

Dwijadas replied, 'Primarily to talk about the Kailash pilgrimage with her aunts. Also to take you back to Balarampur. Please make sure you don't say no to that.'

'Fine, I will go.'

Dwijadas continued, 'In Ma's presence, I cannot really call you Miss Ray. Being the younger sister of Boudie, you must also be younger than me. I will call you by your name, but please do not create an issue over that.'

Bandana laughed and said, 'Why should I? Please do call me by my name, but how do I address you?'

'Just call me Dijubabu. But calling Dada Mukhujyemashai will not do. Everyone knows him as Baradadababu, and you should call him Baradada. That is your second lesson.'

'Why?'

'You can't learn lessons through argument. You must memorize them first. I will answer your question after you have learnt your lessons—not earlier.'

Bandana said, 'Mukhujyemashai may be taken aback.'

'That's fine. But Ma and Boudie will be delighted and that is important.'

'Fair enough. I accept.'

Bandana took her shoes off at the landing and went into Dayamoyee's room, followed by Dwijadas and Basudeb. Dayamoyee was busy with an open steel trunk, and Annada, standing near her, was perhaps giving her a report on the affairs of the household. Dayamoyee looked up and asked Bandana, 'Have you had a wash and change of clothes, child?'

'Yes, Ma, I have.'

'In that case, can you please go and have a look at the kitchen? I do not know what the cook is preparing to serve so many people. After my evening pujas are over, I propose to visit the kitchen.'

Bandana looked at her silently, but she ignored it and told her, 'Diju is not too well. He had nothing to eat when he left this morning. Will you please see to it that his food is prepared early?' And with that, she withdrew to her puja room taking Annada with her.

'What is the matter with you?' Bandana asked.

'Nothing much really. Just a touch of ordinary fever,' replied Dwijadas.

'So what is it you wish to eat now?'

'Whatever you offer me, except sago and barley water.'

Bandana asked, 'If I go to the kitchen, will that lead to any problem?'

Dwijadas said, 'No, I do not think so. Annadadidi must have given you a clean chit. Mother cannot shrug off her suggestions; she is very fond of her. Perhaps, you are no longer stigmatized as a polluted person.'

Bandana paused and then said, 'Very astonishing!'

Dwijadas agreed and said, 'Yes. And while I don't know what you have done or what Annadadidi has told Ma, today I am even more amazed than you are. But, please, don't delay any further. Go and make the arrangements for food. See you soon.'

With that, both of them came out of Ma's room.

TWELVE

Dayamoyee's two aunts, having come to know about the hazards of journeying along on an almost inaccessible route to Kailash, backed out, and Dayamoyee's eagerness also petered out. So her few days in Calcutta were spent in visiting Dakshineshwar, Kalighat, and taking dips in the Ganges. Since the responsibility of work devolves onto hard-working and efficient people, practically, the entire responsibility of running the house was left in Bandana's hands. Sati did not do much. She pushed her sister into everything that had to be done, and, as for herself, she accompanied her mother-in-law everywhere. Even so, whenever they went out, Sati pressed Bandana to come along with them. 'When you are with us, we have no need to ask anybody anything.'

Bipradas could not return home to Balarampur, as he was detained by various engagements in Calcutta and, on top of that, his mother stopped him from returning on the pretext that if he left, there would be no one to escort her home. Returning from a trip to Victoria Memorial one evening, Dayamoyee sent for Bipradas and gushed, 'Whatever you might say, Bipin, educated women are a class apart.'

Guessing correctly that it must be something to do with Bandana, he asked, 'Why, what happened?'

Dayamoyee said, 'You ask what happened? This evening, a huge, red-faced sergeant stopped our car. Fortunately, this girl was with us. She spoke to this sergeant in English, and he promptly let us go. Otherwise, what would have happened to us? Instead of letting us go, he would have probably taken us to the police station—what a disaster! Your new chauffeur is a total washout.'

Bipradas asked, 'Was there a collision?'

Dayamoyee nodded her head in confirmation just as Bandana arrived. Then, she spoke effusively, 'I was just talking about you to Bipin, dear child, that educated women are a class apart. We would have been in great trouble today had you not been with us. The fault was entirely of that English woman. Doesn't know how to drive, yet will insist on doing so just to show off.'

Bipradas smiled as he said, 'Ma, that is the manner of refined women. I am sure that the English woman was an educated person.'

Ma and Bandana both laughed. Bandana remarked, 'Mukhujyemashai, it was the fault of the English woman, not of her education. Ma, let me go to the kitchen to have a look. The cook yesterday did not make Dijubabu's roti soft.'

Looking affectionately at her for a while, Dayamoyee said, 'She keeps an eye on everything. There is nothing that she does not know. And how sweetly she speaks! I feel relieved leaving everything to her—I do not have to do anything.'

Bipradas asked, 'So, you do not resent her as an outcaste?'

Dayamoyee said, 'You keep harping on this. Why should she be an outcaste? Just because her mother went to England once, people dubbed her as a memsahib. Her mother was a woman of a Bengali family just as we are. Bandana wears shoes, so what is wrong with that? Everybody does in foreign countries. She comes out publicly—nothing wrong with it. It is not customary to cover one's head with a veil in Bombay. She just does what she had been taught as a young child. There is no difference between my bouma and her—both are same. She says she will go back with her father, and that makes me unhappy.'

Bipradas said, 'But what is the point in being unhappy? She did not come here to stay. She will have to return in a few days.'

Dayamoyee said, 'Yes, I know, but I do not like the thought of letting her go. I would like to keep her for all time.'

Bipradas said, 'But that is not at all likely. Don't get attached to someone else's child. It is just right that she is here for a short stay.'

Dayamoyee did not take to heart what Bipradas said. Nobody apparently gave much thought of going back to Balarampur. Their days in Calcutta flew by in a festive mood—with talks, laughs, outings, and sightseeing. No one had ever seen Dayamoyee in such a light mood. A bottled-up desire for gaiety apparently opened up, which tended to drown her age-related and natural sense of sobriety. Sati and she occasionally had talks loaded with hints and signs, which only they understood. Perhaps, there was another person who had some inkling—and that was Annada.

The barrister sahib from Punjab and his wife went back home. Both had the same name—Basanta. Dayamoyee made fun of it before they left and extracted a promise that on their return, they must look them up either in Calcutta or in Balarampur. Raysahib's foot injury got better, and he was planning to leave for Bombay the following week. Dayamoyee secured his permission for Bandana to stay back for sometime in Calcutta, followed by a month's stay with her didi at Balarampur.

Pending lawsuits at the high court were a regular feature of the Mukhujye family, and, since the date of hearing of a major case was incumbent, Bipradas had decided to stay on till then. His many engagements in the city often took him out of home. Taking advantage of a Sunday, Dayamoyee approached him and asked, 'Have you heard of this amusing tale, Bipin?'

Bipradas was going through some legal documents. He rose from his chair and asked, 'What amusing tale?'

Dayamoyee said, 'There was some kind of a meeting of protest which the police had banned, but the protesters were adamant. Some sort of violence was inevitable, which scared me stiff.'

'Has Diju gone there?'

'No, that is what I came to tell you. He would not listen to anyone, not even to his boudie. But finally, he listened to Bandana apparently.'

However funny the tale might be, Bipradas felt that it had dented a little of his mother's sense of self-respect. He did not betray his own amazement. He just said, 'Really?'

Dayamoyee replied with a smile, 'That is what I found out. Apparently, they had made a pact, I do not know when, that one of them must forgo wearing shoes here and will not violate the rules of this house, and, in exchange, the other party must listen to what that person says. Bandana, I believe, walked into his room and told him, "Do you remember our pact, Dijubabu? No way can you go to this meeting," and Diju conceded. That was a relief to me. One never knows what kind of trouble he could get into, particularly now that your father is no longer with us.'

Bipradas remained quiet, but Ma continued, 'Earlier, he was busy with his school and college, his studies and tests—all these are now over and done with. Since he has nothing to do, he could land up in all sorts of trouble. I fear that he might turn out to be a disgrace to his reputed family.'

Bipradas smiled and said, 'Have no worries, Ma. Diju will never do anything disgraceful.'

Dayamoyee was still not convinced. 'Suppose he lands himself in jail. Is that not a fearful possibility?'

Bipradas said, 'I agree that could happen. But Ma, ignominy lies not in the act of going to jail, but in what you do to get there. Suppose I am sent to jail for some reason—that is always a possibility—would you be ashamed of me then, Ma? Will you then say that your Bipin is a disgrace to the family?'

Bipradas's statement cut Dayamoyee like a whiplash. Did it carry a latent hint? She had brought up this son, and she well knew that there was nothing that he would not do in the interest of truth and justice. He never bothered about the risks involved when protesting injustice. When he was just eighteen, he was so involved in fighting alone for a Muslim family that it was still a matter of surprise to her that he returned alive. Having heard from Bandana about the incident in the train, she had been speechless with fear. She had worries for Diju, true, but she was much more concerned for her elder son. She was mulling over the thought in her mind when Bipradas asked her, 'So, Ma, are you free from your fear of disgrace? But jail can indeed happen to me any day.'

Dayamoyee anxiously exclaimed, 'Heaven forbid! Please don't say such ominous things. How can you be sent to jail as long as I am alive? Why do I pray for so long to my gods? And what good will all this vast property do for us? I will sell off everything, rather than allow such a disaster to occur.'

Bipradas bent down and touched her feet, and Dayamoyee drew him close to her. She said, 'Whatever happens to Diju will happen, but if you are out of my sight, know it for certain that I will drown myself in the Ganges. No way can I survive it.' As she said this, tears rolled down her face.

'Ma, for this evening...' Bandana entered as he was saying it. Releasing Bipradas, Dayamoyee dried her eyes and, seeing Bandana's bemused face, told her, 'I haven't held him close to me for far too long. I just wanted to do so now.'

Bandana said teasingly, 'A grown-up, old boy—I will tell everyone.'

Dayamoyee protested, 'Do that, but don't call him old. It does not seem all that long ago that I had just arrived as a new bride. Even before I entered the house, an aunt-in-law, then alive, thrust Bipin in my arms and told me, "This is your first child, Bouma. In the rush of the events around the marriage, I don't think the child has been fed for sometime. Go and feed him first and put him to sleep. Everything else can wait." She perhaps wanted to test me if I could do this. I do not know if I passed this test.' She smiled when she said that.

'So, what did you do then?' asked Bandana.

Dayamoyee continued, 'Through my veil, I saw a live doll made of gold looking at me with his eyes wide open. There were still a lot of rituals to go through, but I ran off with the child in my arms. Everyone there made a huge clamour, but I did not listen to anyone. I had no idea where to go, but the maid servant who followed me showed me the child's room. I told her to bring me the child's milk bowl and the feeding spoon. I was not going to stir from my place until I fed him and put him to sleep. Many women in the neighbourhood called me shameless, but I was not bothered. I told myself to let them say whatever they wanted, but no one could take my little jewel away. And you call this child of mine old!'

Recalling a thirty-year-old incident through tears and smiles, Dayamoyee's face looked divine to Bandana. She had never before had the opportunity to appreciate the depth of genuine love that she witnessed at that moment. Bandana looked at Dayamoyee with curious eyes. Then, before checking her emotions, she asked with a small laugh, 'Tell me the truth, Ma. Of your two sons, who is your favourite?'

Dayamoyee parried the question, 'Our scriptures forbid us to spell out the bitter truth.'

Bandana was an outsider, one only recently introduced to them, so Bipradas found the recalling of their past uncomfortable. 'Even if Ma did tell you, you will never appreciate it sensibly. These issues do not feature in the English texts of your college, and you will find it very strange if you try to reconcile what Ma said with your book theories. It would be better not to discuss this.'

It annoyed Bandana. She retorted, 'Mukhujyemashai, you have also read a lot of English books, so how do you understand it?'

Bipradas said, 'Who says we understand our mother? Such ideas occur only in this mother's books. The language, the alphabets, the grammar, they are all different. Only she knows, no one else. But Ma, you came to speak to me about something. What is it?'

Bandana took the hint. 'Ma, I came to ask you about tonight's meal. I am off now, but do come soon. Please, do not go on dreaming with your son in your arms.' With an impish look at Bipradas, she left.

A shadow of anxiety marked Dayamoyee's face. She said in a hesitant voice, 'Bipin, being an upright man, you ought not to deceive your mother ever.'

'For heaven's sake, Ma, what is this prelude for? What is it that you wish to know?'

'Why did you say that you can also be sent to jail? I have not yet abandoned the idea of visiting Kailash, but as of now, I cannot move out even one step.'

Bipradas's face broke into a smile. 'I am not particularly anxious to see you go to Kailash, and don't blame me for that. What I said about my going to jail was just by way of an illustration. I wanted you to appreciate that Diju going to jail will not constitute a disgrace to the family.'

Dayamoyee was not convinced. 'Do not try to mislead me. You are not someone who talks loosely. Either you have done something or planning to do. Tell me the truth.'

Bipradas countered, 'I have told you the truth, but so many cross-currents of thoughts run through one's mind that it is not possible to identify them correctly.'

Dayamoyee said, 'May be, but it is not that. Why is it that whenever I see you, I feel a tug in my heart? I brought you up, but should you betray me in this fashion when I am still alive?' She broke into tears.

Bipradas said, a little disturbed, 'Ma, how can I help if you feel scared of a non-existent disaster in your imagination? Ma, you do know that I can never do anything that will make you unhappy.'

Dayamoyee nodded, 'Yes, I do know that, but why did you ask Diju to take over all your responsibilities?'

'He is old enough. Should he not help me?'

Dayamoyee then was really annoyed. 'Is he capable enough? Don't try to fool me. Are you so fatigued now that you need his help? Be clear about what is in your mind.'

Bipradas kept quiet. He did not remind her that she had in fact asked him to give some thought to Diju's future. Dayamoyee's next words carried a broad hint of that. She said, 'Our home believes in virtue and in piety; no deviance is acceptable. Our life is strictly regulated. I got you married when you were just eighteen years old—not with your consent—but just because we wished it. But Diju says he is not going to get married, he has his MA, and that he is mature enough to know what is or what is not good for him. No one can force him to do anything. If he does not get married, I cannot agree to let him look after my father-in-law's property.'

'When did Diju tell you that he does not wish to get married?' asked Bipradas.

'He often does so. He says that there is no dearth of people willing to marry. Let them marry. He would devote his life to the service of the country. And now you used the example of the jail to put fear into me. Could you not have thought of any other example?'

Bipradas said, 'Why don't you ask his boudie to speak to him?'

'He won't even listen to her.'

'He will when the time comes. If you ask me, I can fix a match for him.'

Just then, Bandana walked in and complained, 'Ma, I have been waiting for you in the kitchen, but you never came.'

'I know. I will be with you in just a minute.'

Bipradas continued, 'Do you remember that daughter of Akshaybabu? She is grown up now, and her accomplishments are matched by her looks. A very acceptable family. If you agree, I can speak to Akshaybabu. I feel sure that Diju will not demur.'

'No, not immediately,' she looked at Bandana as she said this. 'I must talk to Sati before making a move.'

Bandana opened her mouth. She looked at both of them and said, 'What is wrong with it, Ma? I believe the family lives just round the corner; let us take Didi and meet this girl.'

Though not comfortable with the suggestion, Dayamoyee was not sure what to say.

Bipradas seemed keen. 'A good idea. Akshaybabu is a deeply devoted religious person and a scholarly Brahmin. He is a professor of Sanskrit and, though he did not send his daughter to a school or college, he taught her privately at home with great care. I was once invited to their home where I had an opportunity to talk to the girl. The father has named the girl Maitreyee—a very apt name I felt. So, Ma, why don't you go and have a look at the girl? At least, your bouma will concede that there are other good-looking women in this world besides her.'

Ma felt like laughing, but did not; nor did she have anything to say. Bandana insisted, 'Ma, let us go and meet this girl. It is not very far from here.'

Dayamoyee looked at Bandana and noticed a dark shadow cross her face. Dayamoyee then found her tongue and said, 'I know it is not far off, but I have no time now. I must visit the kitchen and fix the menu for tonight's dinner. Come with me.' And then she led Bandana out of the room.

THIRTEEN

After his evening puja, Bipradas went into the library room to look at some papers that had arrived by the morning mail when, unexpectedly, Dayamoyee came in and said, 'You do exaggerate, Bipin, do you not?'

Bipradas got up from his chair and asked, 'Why, Ma?'

'We went to see Akshaybabu's daughter.'

'Is she not good enough?'

Dayamoyee appeared to be in two minds before she spoke, 'No, I would not say so. True, one does not usually come across such a girl, but how could you compare her with my bouma? Leave alone Bouma, she can't even hold a candle to Bandana's good looks.'

Surprised, Bipradas said, 'You must have seen some other girl, not Maitreyee.'

Dayamoyee smiled, 'If you say so, but we did have a long talk with her. She and Bandana had some discussions about books and education, and now you say we must have seen someone else!'

Bipradas argued, 'Possibly, that girl could not respond adequately to Bandana's queries, but, Ma, please don't forget that Bandana is very well read and has passed so many examinations, while this girl has been merely taught at home by her father. The sort of difference between your younger son and me.'

Dayamoyee, highly amused, cautioned Bipradas, 'Hush, Bipin, hush. Diju is in the next room. If he hears you, he will be so mortified that he will run away from home.' She resumed after a pause, 'Your mother may be unlettered, but she is not such a fool that she would regard anyone with a college education to be the best. No, it is not so. On the contrary, the girl quite effectively dealt with Bandana's points. In the car, while coming home, Bandana heaped praises on the girl. My point is why do we need such a well-educated girl in our middle-class family? We shall be quite happy to have someone like Bouma. We cannot have someone who will be arrogant about her education and slight her elders.'

Bipradas felt that his mother was getting confused. He said, 'Have no such fear, Mother. In fact, the less educated one is, the haughtier one gets. If that girl has truly learnt anything from her father, you will find her humble and respectful.'

Dayamoyee found Bipradas's point valid. In reply, she said, 'Granted, but how can we assume that it will indeed be so? Anyway, in our village, who is going to question the educational attainment of brides? On the other hand, those who come to meet the new bride will contemptuously comment that the old hag must have gone blind that she would bring home this bride compared to her lovely elder daughter-in-law. That will be too much for me to stand.'

'But we need to tell Akshaybabu of our decision. I had told him that I did not think you will disapprove.'

Dayamoyee was uncomfortable. She said, 'I wish you had not told him so. Anyway, let me check with Bouma. Let me first get her perspective. We can speak later to Akshaybabu.'

Bipradas said, 'Akshaybabu is a reasonably close relation. But since we had had no contact for a long time, we had become strangers. But putting that aside, I do wonder that since you were not bothered about anybody else's views when you got your elder son married, why are you so concerned now?'

She smiled, 'I am an old woman now, and how long can I go on? How can I get him married without his knowledge to a person with whom he would have to live all his life? You must give me more time to ponder.'

Saying that, she left. But instead of going to her room, she proceeded to meet Bandana's father. Having known him for a few days by then, she felt free to call on him. It was almost evening then, yet she deferred her puja. As she entered his room, she found a young man clad in western clothes, talking to Bandana. Ill at ease, she tried to retreat her steps when Raysahib stopped her. 'Where are you off to, Beyan? He is our Sudhir, he is just like your son. Sudhir, she is the mother-in-law of my niece, Sati; mother of Bipradas. Go, touch her feet.' Sudhir, poor man, was not used to touching people's feet, nor was it easy to do so given his clothing. Nevertheless, he bowed his head down and made a show of it.

In order to explain to Dayamoyee how the young man was like her son, Raysahib went on, 'His father and I were students in England and, since then, we have been very close friends. Sudhir himself has acquired a number of degrees in England, and is presently doing a good job in the education department in Madras. It has been agreed that after their marriage, Bandana and he would go to England and, if they wish, Bandana may go to a college there for further studies, or they may return after visiting some countries. I say, Sudhir, if you can manage to leave in August this year, I can take leave for three months and travel with you. Would it not be nice, Bandana?'

'Of course, Father, it will be wonderful with you there,' agreed Bandana.

A much-enthused Raysahib carried on, 'This will give me some leeway. After your marriage, I will have a month's time to make my plans. No need to rush. Do you follow me, Sudhir?'

Both Bandana and Sudhir nodded in agreement. It then dawned on Dayamoyee that the young man was the future son-in-law of Raysahib. She was shaken for an instant, but the chatelaine of the great Mukhujye family quickly regained her self-control and asked the young man, 'Where is your home, Sudhir?'

Sudhir said, 'Presently in Bombay, but I gathered from my father that our earlier home was in Durgapur. It is unlikely that any trace of ours is left there.'

'Which Durgapur, Sudhir? Of Burdwan district?'

Sudhir confirmed, 'Yes, so I was told by my father. A small village close to Kalna, but I understand that the village has now been ravaged by malaria.'

Dayamoyee, after some reflection, asked, 'Can you tell me your father's name, Sudhir?'

'Sriram Chandra Basu,' replied Sudhir.

With a start, she asked, 'Was your grandfather's name Harihar Basu?'

Raysahib appeared puzzled. He asked, 'Do you know them?'

'Yes, I do. Durgapur happens to be my maternal uncle's home. I was brought up by my grandmother, so I know most people of that village. Their home was in our neighbourhood. But sorry, Sudhir, I must go now as I am late for my evening puja, but please do not go away without having something to eat.'

Sudhir said with a smile, 'That is over and done with. Bipradasbabu had already seen to that.'

'Oh, has he? Well, in that case, I will leave you.' Dayamoyee went away. All the while, she did not look at Bandana nor speak to her.

The next morning, Bipradas went as usual to his mother's room to touch her feet. As he entered her room, he found that there was some packing going on.

'Are you off somewhere?' he asked.

Dayamoyee replied, 'I couldn't find you in the morning, so I asked Dattamashai who told me that if I catch the 9:30 train in the morning, we will reach home before evening. I know you are busy presently with an important court case the day after, so you cannot take us. Do tell Diju to escort us.'

To Bipradas, his mother looked unhappy with her eyes red, giving the impression that she had passed a disturbed night.

He was alarmed and asked, 'Is there an emergency, Ma?'

She replied, 'I meant to visit here for only two days, but I have been here for almost ten. Meanwhile, I have no idea if, during my absence, my puja room with all the deities are being properly looked after. Before I left, I was told that some of our cows were about to calve, and I have no clue what is the situation there. And, on top of that, Basudeb is missing his school. No, Bipin, I cannot afford to tarry here any longer.'

Bipradas knew that they were not trifling issues for Dayamoyee, but he sensed that she had not told him the real reason behind her move. He asked, 'Must you go today?'

'No, son, don't stop me. If Diju cannot come, please arrange for someone else to accompany us.'

Bipradas agreed to do so and, having touched his mother's feet, went to his own room. He found Sati occupied, getting baskets of fruits, sweets, and milk ready for her son, assisted by Annada.

Sati stood up and covered her head. Bipradas asked, 'Annadadidi, any idea what has happened?'

'No, Dada, none. Ma sent for me early this morning and told me that she would leave by the 9:30 train this morning, and that I should arrange food for Boudi and the child.'

Bipradas asked Sati if she knew anything. She shook her head.

Bipradas was baffled. Annada might not know, but how was it that even her daughter-in-law had no clue? He felt deeply concerned. This was so contrary to his mother's nature. Who knew what pain lay behind her unusual action, which she had not disclosed to anyone?

By the time Dayamoyee came downstairs, there was still enough time enough to catch her train. But she seemed very impatient that day. She was keen to get away as soon as possible. Observing Bipradas carrying his bag, she asked anxiously, 'But where is Diju?'

'He is not going, so I will come with you.'

'Did he not agree to go?'

Bipradas said disapprovingly, 'You should not cast aspersions about him in this way. When has he ever been disobedient to you?'

'Then why is he not coming?'

'Nothing really. I never asked him, as I wanted to see for myself what had happened to your deities, your cows—and that is it.' On another occasion, Dayamoyee would have been merely amused and talked to her son about many things, but on that day, she kept quiet.

Annada had gone to tell Bandana, who, having taken her bath just then, was proceeding to see her father. She rapidly went down and was staggered by what she saw. Dayamoyee told her, 'We are going home, Bandana.'

'Going home? Has anything happened there, Ma?'

'No, nothing. I came here for two days, but it has been about ten to twelve days now. I can't stay back any longer. Sadly, I could not wait to see your father—he was not up—please give him my apologies. Diju is here, so is Annada. Please see that good care is taken of your father. Come, Bouma. It is time to leave.' She climbed into the waiting car.

Sati, who was standing close behind, hugged her sister and broke down. She just said, 'We have to go.' She followed her mother-in-law into the car while drying her tears.

Bandana stood rigidly, wondering what had gone wrong.

When Basu came to say farewell to her, she realized that she had not observed the formalities. She went near the car and touched Sati's and Dayamoyee's feet. Sati touched her chin by way of benediction, and Dayamoyee muttered something that was not clear. The car started.

Annada spoke to her tenderly, 'Let's go up, Didi.' Her affectionate voice helped Bandana to shake off her discomposure. She said, 'Annada, please go ahead. Let me go to the kitchen and see the situation now.'

Only last afternoon, it had been agreed that after Raysahib left for Bombay, the rest of them would set out for Balarampur. It apparently was forgotten, as no one talked about it that day; there was not even a verbal invitation for a future visit.

After about an hour, Bandana walked into her father's room carrying tea. He seemed apologetic and said with regret that he missed meeting Dayamoyee. Bandana asked, 'When are we leaving?'

Raysahib asked in return, 'Were you not supposed also to go to Balarampur? Why did you not?'

'How can I go leaving you alone? You are not fully fit yet.'

'I am fine now. Since I gave my word to Beyan that you will go with them, I suggest that I escort you to Balarampur on my way to Bombay. What do you say to that?'

'That can't be, Father. I can't let you travel so far all by yourself.'

Raysahib was delighted by his daughter's concern for him. Nevertheless, deliberately adopting a critical voice, he said,

'No, no. When Beyan sees you, she will mock you that you cannot let your father out of sight. What a shame!'

'Dear Father, have your breakfast. I will be back.'

FOURTEEN

Later in the evening, Bandana went to Dwijadas's room and asked, 'Can I come in this once?' The reply came, 'Not just once, but hundreds and thousands—in fact, infinite times. Please, do come in.'

Bandana went in and kept the door wide open. Switching on all the lights, she drew up a chair near the door and sat down.

Putting aside the book he was reading, Dwijadas sat up on the bed and said, 'What is thy command?'

'What are you reading?'

'A ghost story.'

'What is the priority? Ghost story or guests?'

'Ghost story.'

Bandana was annoyed. She said, 'Making fun of everything is not right. Are you aware that we are guests at your home?'

'I am fully aware that you are guests of my dada; the big chief has commanded that good care should be taken of the guests. I have been so engrossed by this ghost story that it has led to some laxity in my attention to our guests. Do forgive me.'

'Have you any idea how troubled I have been the whole day?'

'I do, positively.'

'Positively? In that case, have you thought of any redress?'

Dwijadas replied, 'I have told you earlier why I haven't. And, secondly, the remedy is beyond me.'

'Why?'

'Because I ought not to talk about it.'

Bandana asked, 'Why did Ma and Mejdi so abruptly return home?'

'It was no fault of Mejdi. She had to, under the command of her all-powerful mother-in-law.'

'But why did Ma go?'

'Only she knows that.'

'And you know nothing?'

Dwijadas said, 'Well, it will not be entirely true if I say I know nothing at all. Boudie had a guess and she shared a little bit of that with me.'

'In that case, you have to tell me that little bit,' said Bandana.

Dwijadas pondered for an instant and said, 'Now you are getting me into trouble. Do you have to know it?'

'Yes, and you have to tell me.'

'Why don't you forget it?'

Bandana protested, 'Dijubabu, you will recall that we had made a pact that in this house I will listen to everything you tell me, and that you will listen to what I say. And you know that I have not violated any of your instructions.' She had tears in her eyes as she said this, but she managed to control herself.

The tears disheartened Dwijadas. He said, 'It is such a pointless matter that I did not wish to tell you. Ma left because she was angry with you, but you are not really at fault. It is entirely Ma's own doing. Boudie may be partly at fault, I suspect. If not directly, then indirectly; as she was a party to this scheme. Dwijadas is totally innocent in this affair.'

Bandana was impatient. 'Why not tell me quickly what this scheme was about?'

Dwijadas replied, 'Perhaps, "scheme" is not the appropriate word. Ma was expecting a development; but when her calculations misfired, she became upset with everything. Perhaps not upset, but frustrated by the failure of her hopes.'

Bandana looked on blankly. Dwijadas continued, 'I am sure you know that Ma's deep aversion for you later turned into deep affection for you. To her, other than you, there is no one who can equal Boudie in looks, learning, intelligence, work efficiency, graciousness, and kindness. Who dares call you an outcaste? If anybody did, Ma would immediately take up cudgels on your behalf, trying to prove that in the whole country, no one would find a more orthodox and devout Brahmin girl like you.' Dwijadas roared with laughter at his own joke.

Though the joke was not quite to her taste, it did not stop her from joining in that laughter.

Dwijadas said, 'Why are you laughing, Bandana? What I told you is at the root of all this crisis.'

Bandana was curious, 'But why?'

Dwijadas carried on, 'In that case, pay attention to me. Dayamoyee has two sons—the elder and the younger. As much as she finds her elder son full of promise and dependable, in the same way she believes that in the whole world, there is no one as incompetent as her younger son. But being a mother, she cannot abandon him. To her, the way to redeem her son is to put the responsibility for him squarely on your shoulders, which will safely see him through life's perilous path. But God disposed otherwise. Yesterday evening, she discovered that your shoulders were not available—no room there at all—meaning that all Dayamoyee's resolutions and dreams were shattered by one Sudhirchandra who has occupied that space. Who can dislodge him?' Once again, he roared with laughter.

Bandana asked, 'May I know the meaning of this roaring laughter? Is it because of Ma's discomfiture or a sense of your personal relief?'

'None of this, though I must confess I did derive some unalloyed pleasure at the image of my mother getting toppled in this fashion. Won't do her any harm; though this episode might teach her that in this world, sagacity is not her monopoly, but that there are others with equal claim. Forget me, but had she confided in Dada about her plan, if nothing else, she could have been spared the unpleasant consequences. Both Dada and I knew you were already engaged to be married, that you were bound with a bond of love, so there was no way to upset this, nor was it desirable to do so.'

'But who told you?'

'Your father. The day we arrived here, Raysahib regaled both of us with the pleasant topic of your love, your engagement, and your forthcoming marriage. No, please, don't get annoyed with him. He is a simple soul, and he could not resist sharing his happiness with his relations.'

After a pause, Bandana asked, 'Is that why Mukhujyemashai asked us to meet Maitreyee?'

Dwijadas said, 'I do not really know, because Dada's innermost thoughts are even beyond the knowledge of the gods. All I know is that according to him, Maitreyee is a supremely accomplished girl, and is in no way unsuitable for the rich and respectable Mukhujye family.'

Bandana asked, 'And may I ask what your views are about Maitreyee?'

Dwijadas said, 'In this family, that is an irrelevant question. I am merely the third party. Whichever girl, the first and the second party, meaning Ma and Dada, choose to pair with me, I have to live with her in supreme bliss. That is the tradition of this family, and it is inflexible.'

The way he said it made Bandana laugh. She said, 'Assuming, for instance, that instead of Maitreyee, they choose Bandana, then what?'

Dwijadas dramatically hit his head and said, 'Alas, Bandana, such a false hope! The wicked Rahu has devoured the full moon, and a Sudhirchandra leaped in from nowhere and set fire to the place. And before Dwijadas's eyes, his golden Lanka was reduced to ashes. Dear lady, no more talk about this, otherwise the heart of this poor fellow will shatter.'

His dramatic talk made Bandana laugh once again. 'But the golden Lanka was not entirely burnt down. Ashok Kanan was spared. So your heart need not shatter.'

Shaking his head, Dwijadas said, 'That is a pointless assurance. Rama was lucky, but, by all accounts, I am ill-fated. All my hopes have been dashed to the ground—nothing remains.'

'Nothing is lost.'

'What isn't lost?'

Bandana said firmly, 'Nothing. Dwijadas may be unlucky, but Bandana is not. No Sudhirchandra can wreck my destiny. No one can, not even your mother or your dada.'

Her firm yet quiet voice astounded Dwijadas.

Bandana asked, 'Why are you quiet? Are you feigning that you have no idea what my heart wants?'

'I have no wish to mislead you. Yes, I do have a good guess, but, at the same time, I am assailed with doubt.'

'Get rid of those misgivings now. I have no uncertainty in my mind. Do you remember the day I left your home in anger? When, from an upstairs window, you waved farewell to me, we had known each other very briefly. Do you think the significance of that gesture was lost on me?'

Finding him quiet, Bandana asked, 'Are you still nursing your doubts?'

Dwijadas responded, 'Perhaps, a little more push will dispel them, but I wonder if this way of resolving my doubts will persist forever.'

Bandana observed, 'Let the situation that allows a forever arrive, then we can see to it. But I have no way of convincing someone who chooses to be sceptic.'

'Not me, but my mother. How do I explain this to her?'

Bandana said, 'Your mother will understand herself. She loves me like her own daughter. She left somewhat disturbed, but if I cannot convince her, then what hope do I have? But I am not worried, for I am sure that someday I will be able to convince her.' As she said that, her voice choked and she had tears in her eyes.

Swinging between the truth and the untruth, Dwijadas was not initially free of doubt; but her tears and the change in her voice effectively did that. It was no joke. Pained and bewildered, he exclaimed, 'What is this Bandana, are you crying?'

Bandana dried her eyes and turned round. Dwijadas kept quiet for a while and said, 'But Sudhir has not wronged you, Bandana.'

She did not turn back to face him, but just said, 'What is this talk about wrong and right? I am not here to avenge him, am I?'

Dwijadas did not know how to react. After some reflection, he said, 'Sudhir is someone who belongs to your society, but you will never find the culture of the Mukhujyes compatible. So why do you wish to walk into this sort of a prison for life? For me? You will probably not realize this for the time being; but when you do later, there will be no end to your distress. I have no clue how you have read me, but I am not isolated from Mother, Boudie, Dada, our puja room, our guest house, and our relations—I am one of them. You will never have me all for yourself. Can you reconcile to this on a lifelong basis?'

Bandana said, 'If I cannot abide it, the road to death is always open. No prison can prevent this. I do not also know how you have read me, but I do not wish to have my husband all to myself, away from my sister-in-law, my brother-in-law, my mother-in-law, our puja room, our guest house, and our relations. He will remain mine along with all of them.'

Dwijadas was stunned. He said, 'But Bandana, these cannot be your own ideas. Who taught you this?'

'No one,' Bandana said. 'I learnt all this by watching Ma and Mukhujyemashai in this family in every sphere. Ma is the senior most, next comes Mukhujyemashai, followed by Didi, and then you. Even Annada has her own place in this pantheon. If I ever come to this family, I know I will be junior to all of them; but I will not find that incongruous.'

Dwijadas felt happy as well as dejected after hearing her. He knew that it was improper to elicit Bandana's thoughts in that fashion, and that the discussion had to cease. He hardened his heart before he spoke, 'It will be useless to tell Ma all this. I know she loves you like a daughter and it was her devout wish to bring you to this family as the younger daughter-in-law. She could then have happily proceeded for Kailash after putting her two sons in the hands of you two sisters. In the event of her death, during this difficult journey, she knows that the responsibility of this large home will be secured. But sadly, that is not to be. To her, to be engaged is as good as being married. You may abandon him because you are not ritually married, but to Mother, her son cannot occupy that vacancy.'

Bandana paled with concern. She asked, 'Has your mother really said this?'

Dwijadas said, 'I do not think it impossible that she might have said so. According to Boudie, what had hurt her the most is that Sudhir is not the same caste as us. We know that you do not believe in the caste system, but to Mother, this is such a huge barrier that it cannot be ignored.'

'And do you also share this view?'

'Did I not tell you that I am the third party? It does not matter what I think.'

Bandana got up, as it was time for her father's dinner. Before leaving, she said, 'Father's leave is over, so he will return to Bombay tomorrow. Shall I go back with him?'

Dwijadas said, 'It is not for me to decide, but if you go, please do not misunderstand me. After you go, I will tell Ma everything candidly on your behalf. What will remain thereafter is the memory of this evening.'

Bandana quietly left the room without saying anything.

FIFTEEN

Back in her room, Bandana felt mortified. Was she inebriated to have exposed her heart and frittered away her dignity like a shameless supplicant? And Dwijadas, being a man, remained shrouded in mystery. His face did not reveal denial or happiness; neither did he show hope nor comfort. On the contrary, he repeatedly joked that he was merely the third party. His wishes in that home were irrelevant. But that was not all. In his mother's name, she was told that her engagement was tantamount to marriage, and Dayamoyee's son could not fill the position left vacant by Sudhir. But her cup of humiliation was not yet full. Seeing tears in her eyes, he had kindly relented to relate Bandana's shameless story to his mother.

That was not the end of the story. In reply to Dwijadas, she, on her own, offered to come into the family as the junior-most member. She had really demeaned herself, so much so that even committing suicide could not redeem that degradation.

She received a message that her father wanted to see her. Through her insistence, she got her father to agree that they would leave for Bombay the next day. It had been earlier decided to catch the night train on the day Bipradas returned. Raysahib was not too happy to go away in this fashion, but he had to because of his daughter's wishes.

Bandana lay down in her bed in low spirits, eventually falling asleep. Early in the morning, she got up and completed packing for her father and then for herself. She made reservations for the railway journey by telephone and sent a cable to Bombay. The departure time was in the evening, but she was impatient to get away.

Annada came in about 9:00 in the morning and, watching the goings-on, asked, 'Why, what is up?'

Bandana said while packing, 'We are leaving tonight.'

'But surely, not today. You are supposed to leave tomorrow.'

'No, tonight,' said Bandana and resumed her packing.

Annada said, 'Then let me help you, Didi.'

'Don't bother. Better get back to your work.' She seemed to resent everyone in that house.

Though Annada did not know what happened, she suspected a tension somewhere. All of a sudden, Ma had returned home yesterday, and equally abruptly, Bandana was going away that day. Being a decent soul, she said with some hesitation, 'It is my fault, Didimoni, I got up late.'

Bandana looked up and said, 'You don't have to give me any explanation, Annada. You can do that to your employer if you feel like. Dijubabu is in his room, go and tell him.' She knew that as an only child, she had been brought up rather indulgently; but she also knew that that did not mean that she was allowed to speak so roughly. She had probably never spoken to anyone in such a manner, and she felt very upset about it. It was Annada who spoke softly, 'It was nearly dawn by the time the doctors left when I decided to go back to bed. Instead, I sat down resting my back against the wall, and did not know when my eyes shut and how time flew. You talked about my employer, but are you not also one? Have I given you any offence? Do let me help you.'

Bandana had not been paying any heed to Annada till then, but the word 'doctors' pricked her ears. She looked at her and asked, 'What do you mean by the doctors left?'

Annada said, 'Last night, Diju was very unwell. He has not been well since he arrived here, but he does not care. When it was decided that he was to accompany Mother to home yesterday, he sent for me and said, "Please, don't tell Mother, but inform Dada and excuse my inability to go. Anudidi, I feel very weak. I can't even stand up."

'I have raised him since he was a little boy. He tells me everything. I was scared and said, "If you are not well, why are you keeping it to yourself?" It is his nature to laugh away everything. He told me, "Didi, see them off. You will find me up and about then." I know he does not get along with his mother and does not go anywhere with her, so I thought this must be a ruse to avoid going with her. Barababu left with them, and he spent the whole day in bed and ate nothing. I went to see him in the afternoon to ask him how he was, and he said he was fine. Looking at him, I did not think so. I suggested sending for a doctor, but he ruled that out. "Why do you want to waste Dada's money? If she comes to hear of this, the big lady will be very upset." He has never gotten over his grievance against his mother. He went without food the whole day and stayed in bed, so I asked, "If you are really well, then why are you staying in bed?" He laughed me away, and said that according to our scriptures, nothing was more virtuous than being in bed, as it leads to salvation, so he was trying to earn some merits for the next world. Making fun as usual. But it left me deeply concerned about him.'

After a pause, she resumed, 'It was close to midnight when there was a knock on my door. It was Diju. Why did he come to see me so late at night? I went out and was shocked by his looks—sunken eyes, broken voice, body shivering, but with his usual smile. "Didi," he said, "you raised me, so I woke you up. If I must die, then I want to do so with my head on your lap."' Annada broke into tears. When she collected herself, she said, 'I took him to his room. He kept throwing up and had a severe stomach ache. I was afraid that he might not last the night. Doctors were sent for, and they came and gave him an injection and we applied hot-water fomentation all night. Early in the morning, Diju fell asleep. The doctors said that the crisis was over. For me, it was a nightmare.' She once again broke down.

Bandana was deeply moved, 'Why did you not wake me up, Annada?'

Annada said, 'You had that problem in the morning, so I did not wish to disturb you. Diju did tell me to inform you.'

'How is he now?'

'Better, and still sleeping. He might do so until the evening, the doctors say. We are all waiting for Barababu to return.'

'Has he been informed?'

'Dattamashai says there is no need for that. He is due back soon in any case.'

'Are there any attendants in his room?'

'Yes, Didi, two of them.'

'When are the doctors coming to see him again?'

'Around evening. There is no problem now.'

The doctors' assurance was the only comfort for Bandana. There was nothing that she could do.

Bandana told her father about Dwijadas's illness. He was anxious. 'I was not told anything!'

'They did not want to disturb our sleep.'

'But that was not right.' A little later, he told her, 'Someone has gone to get our tickets. Berths have already been reserved, but now, there seems to be a problem in our departure.'

Bandana said, 'Why should there be a problem? What good can we do if we stay back?'

'No, we are not doing any good, yet...'

'No, Father, no. We are being constantly held up. Please do not change your mind again.'

A couple of hours were still left before their departure when Annada came to Bandana's room. Bandana asked, 'Is Dijubabu well?'

'Yes, Didi, he is and still asleep.'

Bandana said, 'He will probably be still sleeping by the time we leave, and we shall be away by the time the others return.'

Annada nodded in agreement, 'It will be 9:00 a.m. when

Barababu returns. We will heave a sigh of relief when he is here. Till then, we will continue to be anxious.'

'But why, Annada? There is no cause for anxiety now.'

Annada agreed, 'True, there is no fear now. But with Barababu at home, it is a different feeling. No one then has any responsibility. It all devolves on him. He is wise and sensible as well as courageous and sober. We feel we are all comfortably sheltered under a banyan tree.'

The same old story, the same old litany of virtues—characteristics of employers ingrained in the minds of the servants. On another occasion, Bandana might have made some barbed remarks, but not at that moment.

Annada continued, 'But this Diju! The two brothers appear to be poles apart.'

'But why so?' asked Bandana.

Annada said, 'It is so, Didi. Diju has no responsibilities, no involvements, and no sobriety. Boudie says he is like the autumn cloud—gives no water and discharges no lightning. He floats round and regardless of how serious the situation is, he carries on with a light heart. He is neither a home bird, nor an ascetic. Countless number of borrowers have saved themselves by persuading him to write off their loans.'

Bandana asked, 'Doesn't Mukhujyemashai get indignant?'

'He does, of course. And his mother even more so. But where can they get hold of him? He has a knack of suddenly going missing until his boudie starts weeping and fretting and people go on a search and bring him back. But this cannot go on and on. Some day, he will get married and have children. If the situation goes on like this, it can only lead to bankruptcy.'

'Why do you not all speak to him then?' asked Bandana.

'We have all spoken to him numerous times, but to no effect. He says, "Why does that worry you? I may get bankrupt, but Boudie won't. All of us will then descend on her."'

Bandana laughed and asked, 'What does Mejdi say to that?'

Annada said, 'She spoils her brother-in-law. She says, "How can we eat while Diju starves? My income of five hundred rupees a month cannot be taken away by anyone. We will manage with that, however humbly. Let Barababu gloat with his millions, we shall not go begging to him."'

Those words delighted Bandana to no end. It was none other than her own cousin who said it; yet, in the environment in which she she lived, no one spoke like that nor even conceived of doing so.

Annada's story sounded like a tale from ancient times. It was a joint family not just for outward show, but in reality—in every way. Annada was just not a paid maidservant, but the didi of Dwijadas. Not just superficially; even at that time, he confided in her. Annada's father had died while working for that family, and her son had grown up there and earned his living by serving the family. Annada did not need anything, yet she could never sever that bond and leave. There must have been countless persons connected with that rich and big family over generations. Dayamoyee's unruly son told her yesterday that he was merely a part of the whole ensemble comprising his mother, his dada, boudie, their many deities, the guest house— Bandana could never have him all by herself away from all these. Bandana did not disbelieve it, but it was only then that she grasped the real significance of that observation.

Bandana would have liked to talk so much more, but was interrupted. Raysahib was getting impatient. It was time for them to leave, and she had to get ready. Her father called for her as he went down. Bandana felt that regardless of her reluctance, they had to leave. The arrangement had been made on her insistence, and in no way could that be changed at that moment. As she left her room, the thought struck her that she would never return to that place where she had a very memorable stay. And she would never forget it. As she passed Dwijadas's room, she looked through the open window but did not see him.

Down where a car was waiting for them, Raysahib gave Dattamashai some money for the servants and left a request to keep him posted about Dwijadas's progress.

Before getting into the car, Bandana drew Annada aside and told her, 'You are Dijubabu's didi. You brought him up. Please take this ring and give it to your daughter-in-law from me.' She took off the ring from her finger and gave it to Annada. The car started and, unconsciously, Bandana looked up at the window, but Dwijadas was not there to bid her adieu. He was unwell and deep in slumber.

SIXTEEN

The direct reproach and indirect humiliation in Dayamoyee's manner towards Bandana had deeply hurt Sati. Since she could not talk back to her mother-in-law, she asked her husband to meet her in the room and handed him a letter to give to Bandana. Bipradas was going to return to Calcutta by the afternoon train. Unexpectedly, Dayamoyee came to her room. This was so unusual that both her son and his wife were nonplussed. Sati was about to leave the room, but Dayamoyee stopped her. 'No, Bouma, don't go. I don't wish to speak ill of your sister behind your back, so wait. Do you know, Bipin, why I rushed back home?'

Bipradas said, 'Not exactly, but I guessed there was a problem.'

Dayamoyee said, 'There could have been, but fortunately there was none. Ma Durga came to our rescue. Beyaimashai would be going back to Bombay tomorrow, and the idea was that Bandana would come here to be with her mejdi for some days. If the girl has any sense, she should not come here, but return to Bombay with her father. If she does not, tell her to do so. Do not be unhappy, Bouma. A girl like that has no place in this home.'

Bipradas kept quiet, much perplexed. Dayamoyee continued, 'It is my misfortune that I became fond of her. I believed that she was one of us. Lapses in her manners, I thought, were due to her education, just transient like flying clouds, which go away with the wind. After all, she is Sati's sister. But she selected a husband from a Kayastha family! How could they stoop so low, being a Brahmin?'

Bipradas said, 'Is that the problem? But Ma, they do not believe in the caste system.'

Dayamoyee said, 'Yes, though I had heard so, I had not really seen it for myself. I did not realize the extent of revulsion one feels until confronted by an actual episode.' She shuddered with aversion. 'Forget it. Who is she to me? Let them do as they wish—but she is barred from this house.'

Finding Bipradas quiet, she asked, 'Have you nothing to say?'

'You did not ask for my views. You just decreed that Bandana could come to this house, and that will be so.'

'Do you think my decree is wrong?'

'Yes, I do, Ma. Bandana has done no wrong. Their social mores are not like ours; they do not subscribe to the caste system. You knew it. In spite of that, you invited her home and grew fond of her. Perhaps, you thought that they just spoke a certain way, but did not practise what they said. That was your mistake, and that is why you are hurt.'

Dayamoyee conceded, 'That may be true, but doesn't the issue of her marriage repulse you?'

Bipradas said calmly, 'She is not yet married; but even so, I ought not to be displeased. Rather, I respect that they practise what they believe. They have not really deceived anyone. I know many in Calcutta who loudly boast that they are non-believers, that they do not accept the caste system, and roundly malign our social customs. But when it is a question of practice in their own lives, they are never to be seen. These are the people for whom I have the strongest contempt. Ma, don't take it badly, but your Diju belongs to this class.'

Not that it made Dayamoyee unhappy, but referring to Diju, she said, 'He is a slacker. But tell me, Bipin, if you do not disapprove of Bandana, why do you then refuse to eat food touched by her? You gave up eating food from our kitchen because I sent her there. Instead, you started eating in my room. Others may not have known the reason, but do you think I did not?'

Bipradas said, 'How could you have become my mother if you do not understand my actions? I do believe in the caste system after all, so how could I eat food touched by her? But the day I renounce my belief, I will openly eat food touched by her. Not clandestinely.'

Dayamoyee said, 'You have no idea, Bipin, how I kept this shielded from her. Whether she comes here or not, please do ensure that she never comes to know the truth. She will be much hurt, and she has great respect for you.' Her last few words were tinged with affection.

Bipradas smiled, 'I have no idea if she has any respect for me, but she was fully aware that I didn't eat food touched by her.'

'Do you mean to say that despite being aware of this, a sensitive girl like her still reveres you so highly? How can that be?'

'You might know whether she reveres me or not, but what I know is that she is extremely intelligent. All your attempts at cover-up were wasted.'

Dayamoyee mused over it for some time and then said, 'Is that why she pressed so hard?'

'What do you mean by press?'

Dayamoyee said, 'Being a widow, I eat only simple food, but she would have none of that. Everyday, she would get all sort of vegetables from the market, cut and clean them, and insist that the cook Bamunpisi prepare at least ten dishes. She well knew that what she could not achieve openly, she could through an agent. Did you not realize, Bipin, that Bamunpisi was incapable of cooking so well?'

Bipradas said, 'No, I can't say that I did, but I did have a sort of suspicion that some items from the main kitchen may have found their way to your kitchen. I am pleased to know that it was no act of God, but deliberate. Anyway, Ma, give me your final decision. I must rush to catch my train. Have you agreed to invite her or not?'

Dayamoyee turned to Sati and asked her, 'What do you say, Bouma?'

When she was younger, Sati did speak to her mother-in-law in her husband's presence, but not in the later days. She usually remained quiet or avoided speaking, but she spoke that day, 'Let us forget it, Ma. It is pointless for her to come here.'

The reply did not suit her mother-in-law. Her intention was for her daughter-in-law to say what she herself could not. So, she teased, 'Ah, so the rich man's daughter is upset?'

'No, I am not upset, but given the way we left yesterday, it will not be proper to ask her here.'

'Why not? If we did something wrong, can that not be remedied?'

'That is not my point. But what is the need? In the past, when she had wanted to visit us, we never agreed because of anticipated problems. These problems are still with us. My husband gave up eating food from our kitchen because she visited there. So why bring her here?'

Bipradas said, 'That should be her grievance, not yours. Even so, Bandana has much regard for me, as Ma will confirm.'

Sati looked up and, forgetting the presence of her mother in-law, said, 'Why only Ma? I can also confirm it. Women are seldom critical of those for whom they have great respect. Women continue to worship the gods who have caused them pain—believing that they go through such pain for their own good.'

She turned to her mother-in-law, 'She also had high regard for you and was very fond of you. You assumed that she arranged for food in your room for the sake of your son, but that was not true. She did it for both of you, being fond of both of you. You put her in charge of the kitchen with the responsibility of feeding all, but she did not provide fancy food to others while you were restricted to your simple fare. That is why, all of us were given the same simple food to eat. Why are we going back

123

and forth about this anyway? Our hopes around her are now lost. She will not be back.' So saying, Sati quickly left the room.

Dayamoyee and Bipradas were both left stunned at that. The things Sati said and the manner in which she said them was so unexpected that they were afraid that she was not fine. 'Is anything wrong, Ma?' Bipradas asked.

'I really do not know, son,' Dayamoyee replied.

'What were your hopes about Bandana? What hopes have been lost?'

Dayamoyee was most disconcerted and could not admit her thoughts. She skirted the issue, 'Not today, Bipin, some other time.'

'Have you given any thought to Akshaybabu's daughter? We owe them an answer.'

'I am not unwilling, but it now depends on all of you. Ask Diju how he feels about it.' She also left the room, leaving Bipradas confused. There were no clear answers, and he did not have time to sort it out before he left.

Returning to Calcutta, Bipradas found the house almost empty. Bandana and her father had left a few hours earlier. Somehow, he had not been prepared for that. All Annada could tell him was that Raysahib was not so keen to leave, but did so at the insistence of his daughter. No one had any claims on Bandana, nor had she any obligation to stay on. Indeed, she was just a guest. Nevertheless, it disturbed Bipradas that she had left in such haste, abandoning an ill and unconscious Dwijadas. It rankled him; he felt like punishing her for her thoughtless and unkind actions. True to his nature, however, he did not express his annoyance.

Four days later, Bipradas returned from the high court, running a high temperature. It could have been malaria or something else. His eyes were red and he had an intense headache. He told Annada, 'Anudi, I do not usually have fevers. I've cheated that demon for a long time, but it seems that he is desperate to do his worst now. Looks like he is determined to make me suffer and not easily let me go.'

Though deeply anxious, Annada spoke reassuringly, 'Have no fear, Dada. You are a man of virtue; no demon can harm you. You will be well soon, but I cannot ignore it. Let me get a doctor.'

'Yes, do that, Anudi,' he agreed and then took to bed.

Annada was troubled. Dwijadas had left for home the previous day on being informed that Basudeb was unwell. Dattamashai had gone to Dhaka on business. She was at a loss as to what could she do by herself. In the morning, she spoke to Bipradas, 'Bipin, will you be cross if I say something?'

'Have I ever been cross with you, Anudi?'

Annada sat down and, while gently massaging his brow, said, 'I can devotedly look after you when you are ill, but being an unlettered woman I know nothing. I cannot send a message home. How can Bouma come, leaving behind a sick child? Can I not send a message to Bandanadidi?'

Bipradas laughed, 'Is Bombay in our neighbourhood that she will be here the instant she gets your message? Forget it.'

Annada said, 'Bandanadidi is in Calcutta. She did not go to Bombay.'

'Bandana is in Calcutta?'

'Yes, at her masi's place in Ballygunge. Her uncle is a renowned doctor in Punjab. They are in Calcutta for their daughter's marriage. They met unexpectedly at the Howrah railway station just when Bandana and her father were about to leave for Bombay. The masi forced them to go to her house. She told them that since they had met so fortuitously, she could not let them return until after their daughter's marriage. Her father stayed back only for a day, but Bandana is still there.'

Bipradas asked, 'Does she know this masi?'

'Yes, her eldest masi. They live far way, so they hardly meet. But are closely related.'

'How do you happen to know all this?'

'They came here yesterday to look in on Diju. I was stitching a garment for my grandson when two cars arrived carrying many people, and among them I spotted Bandanadidi. In her changed clothes, she did not look like our old Bandana. I did not know what to do. Didi came up and asked about everyone. She spoke about herself and that is when I came to know that she was likely to be in town for a month. She said she was having a great time with theatre and film shows, picnics, visits to garden houses, and whatnots—an endless rounds of diversions.'

'Did you tell her about Basudeb's illness?' asked Bipradas.

'I did. She said that it did not sound serious. He will recover soon.'

'So will I, Anudi. So what is the point of informing her? Can't you manage to look after me just for a few days?'

Annada said, 'Of course, I can. Yet, I think that we ought to tell her, or else Bouma may be unhappy. After all, she happens to be her sister.'

Bipradas reflected for a while and then agreed, 'Do so. But I wonder if she will come, sacrificing all those amusements. I don't think so.'

Annada said, 'Nor do I, particularly so because of her new style. Anyway, let us try.'

'Go ahead then,' Bipradas sounded indifferent.

SEVENTEEN

When her masi met Bandana unexpectedly at Howrah station, it was not difficult for her to persuade Bandana to defer her journey to Bombay and instead go back with her. Masi was returning to Calcutta from Punjab, where her husband worked, for their daughter's marriage. Bandana's ready agreement to her masi's proposal was not without a purpose. Bandana had lived far away from home for most of her life, and her education and cultural affiliation were rooted to where she lived then. The bulk of the society to which she belonged was located in Calcutta of which she knew little. Whatever little knowledge she had was derived from books, newspapers, magazines, etc. Another source was reports from people who frequently visited Calcutta—thrilling tales of successful women such as Anita Chatterjee, MA, Binita Bannerjee, BA, etc., also the latest ideas and lifestyles of the twentieth century. But there were no ways of separating fact from fiction. Her present impressions were partly exaggerated and partly distorted as well as vague. Her masi's invitation provided her with the opportunity to closely see various aspects of that society, and she seized the chance.

She met many members of the society and spent a great deal of time with them. Her father, meanwhile, returned to Bombay, whilst Sudhir stayed back. The other day, she and her party had been to a picnic and, on their way back, they dropped in to enquire about Diju.

Masi's home was bustling with constant streams of visitors, and they were occupied with the task of feeding people as well as with discussions about the arrangements for the forthcoming wedding. A tea party had been set up for the evening. Guests were vigorously enjoying the party when Bipradas's large limousine entered the gates. The servants present there were bewildered by the unusually plain dress of the middle-aged woman who came out of the car. It was absolutely incongruous with the limousine. Annada had worn a coarse white borderless sari, a similar coarse body wrap, and no shoes; her wrists were shorn of any ornaments and her veil came down to her eyebrows. She appeared a trifle hesitant. She asked someone, assuming him to be a Bengali, 'Is Bandanadidi home?'

He turned out to be a Bengali and said, 'Yes, she is having tea. Please come inside and sit down.'

'I will wait here. Can you send her a message?'

'I can, but what is the message?'

'Please tell her that one Annada from Bipradasbabu's home is here.'

Bandana came down immediately. Taking Annada by the hand, she took her inside and asked her to take a seat. She seemed to have overlooked that by social standards, the widow ranked pretty low—she was nothing but a maidservant.

For no apparent reason, her eyes were damp. She said, 'I never imagined that you would come to see me. I thought that perhaps all of you have forgotten me.'

'No, Didi, we have not. Barababu sent me to you...'

'No, Anudi. I will not talk to you if you insist on addressing me with the polite "you".'

Annada laughed, 'I use the familiar "you" for them as I brought them up, but I cannot do this to you as I am merely a servant of their house.'

Bandana said, 'I believe Mukhujyemashai has been in Calcutta for nearly a week. Could he not have come himself? I think he knows that I have not gone to Bombay.'

'Yes, he does know, but he is loaded with so much work that he has hardly any spare time.'

The answer did not please Bandana. She said, 'We all have work to do. He sent you out of a sense of decency because we called on them. Do tell him that my masi is nowhere as rich as they are, but he would not have lost his caste if he called in here just for once. Nor would it have dented his high dignity.'

It was not for Annada to respond to such grievances. As she began to request her to visit their home, Bandana cut her short, 'No Anudi, that is not possible. My cousin is getting married the day after tomorrow.'

Annada was in a quandary. What was the appropriate time to speak of Bipradas's health?

Bandana asked her, 'Who suggested that I should go to your house? Dijubabu, I believe, is not here. It must then be Bipradasbabu. Tell him that he has developed a bad habit of ordering people about. I am not one of his debtors, nor am I an employee of his estate. If he wants me to do something, he can ask me himself. Incidentally, how is Mejdi?'

'She is fine.'

'And the others?'

'Little Basudeb is not too well.'

'Basudeb? What is wrong with him?'

'I don't really know.'

Bandana looked worried and said, 'How is it that Bipradasbabu is still here when his son is unwell? Are his legal affairs and his money such a priority for him? He should have some sense of right and wrong.'

Annada said, 'No, Didi, it has nothing to do with his preoccupation with money. He himself has been bedridden for the last two days. I cannot inform his home as they are struggling with his son's illness, and Dattamashai is also not here. He is away in Dhaka on business. I am alone here, an unlettered woman, who is at a loss as to what to do. I pray that whatever is wrong with Bipin does not turn serious. Bipin is hardly ever unwell, and that is what worries me the most. After the wedding is over, can you not manage to visit us at least for once?'

Bandana was alarmed. 'Has a doctor seen him? What does he say?'

'Yes, a doctor has seen him. In his view, there is no cause for alarm. But, at the same time, he advised consulting another doctor.' Annada's eyes filled with tears. She caught hold of Bandana's hands and appealed, 'I will cope somehow for two days, but will you still not come when the wedding is over? Must your displeasure with us continue to prevail so strongly?'

Bandana pondered for a moment and then said, 'Yes, I will. Let us go.'

'Just now?'

'Yes, now.'

'Won't you let someone at the house know? They will be worried.'

'That will delay me, Anudi. Come now.' Bandana went straight to the car, not waiting for Annada to reply. She beckoned to a servant and told him to inform her aunt that she had gone to her mejdi's place where her husband was lying ill.

Daylight had almost faded when she entered Bipradas's room. He was sitting up on his bed, resting against cushions piled up against the wall. He did not look all that ill. Bandana was relieved and said, 'Greetings, Mukhujyemashai. If Mejdi were here, she would have taken offence and reminded me that the proper thing to do was to touch the feet of senior relatives. But I dare not do so, in case my touch sullies you.'

Bipradas just smiled. Bandana said, 'Why have you sent for me? To look after you? Anudi said it was time for your medicines, but what do I see? All these medicines seem to be our modern-day things. Where are the pills from the kaviraj? Who advised you to see a doctor?'

Bipradas said, 'In our parlance, there is a word called "precocious". Do you know what it means?'

Bandana retorted, 'Yes, yes, I do know. They are people who loathe other people so much that they do not touch them. Are there more savagely precocious people than them?'

Bipradas said, 'Yes, there are. There are some people who have no patience with discerning the true from the false; they

132

sting the innocent and take credit for it. You are the leader of that pack.'

'Can you tell me which innocent person I have stung without reason?'

'I don't have to tell you, Bandana. You will know when the time comes.'

'Well, I will wait for that day,' said Bandana and, pulling up a chair near the bed, asked, 'Tell me how you are now.'

'I am well enough, though my temperature may go up at night.'

'Why did you send for me? Why do you need me?'

'I do not need you, but Anudi does. She is nervous. She tells me that your cousin's marriage is set for the day after tomorrow. Do come and see me when it is over. I need to pass on to you your mejdi's message.'

'Can you not do it now?'

'No, not now.'

Bandana remained quiet for a few minutes and then said, 'You are really not all that unwell. You will get well in a couple of days. Even so, I will stay back on the pretext that I need to be here to look after you. I have sent for my luggage; please don't say no to that.'

Bipradas smiled and said, 'Why should I say no? But what about your cousin's marriage?'

'Well, I am not the bride. So my absence will not stop the marriage.'

'But you stayed back in Calcutta just for this.'

Bandana said, 'Not exactly for this. We live far away from home, cut off from our own society. Whatever I know about them is derived from books or from talking to people, but I cannot identify with that society. I felt that we are outcastes. So when Masi invited me for her daughter's wedding, I felt that it was a great opportunity to meet our people. I did not wish to miss the opportunity.'

Bipradas said, 'But the marriage has not taken place yet. So when did you get the opportunity to meet these others of your society?'

'I haven't fully done so, but whatever little I have learned is enough.'

'Can you tell me, Bandana, how much were you able to identify with them?'

It made Bandana laugh. 'Get well. I will give you a full report later.'

The servants came and switched on the lights. Bandana shut the window at the head of the bed, gave him his medicines, and said, 'No more sitting up, you must lie down now.' She made up the bed, smoothed the pillows, and when Bipradas lay down, she covered him with a sheet from his chest down to his feet. She said, 'After you get well, I don't know how much of cow dung and Ganges water you will need to sanctify you.'

He spread out his arms and said, 'So much. But I am amazed to see that you have some knowledge of how to look after people.'

'Only some knowledge? This won't do, Mukhujyemashai. You need to know us better.'

'Meaning?'

'Meaning, if you must revile us, do so with your eyes open. I cannot accept your uninformed criticisms.'

With a mocking smile, Bipradas asked, 'Who are this "us", Bandana, about whom I must be better informed? Are they those from whom you just escaped?'

'Who told you that I escaped?'

'Your face told me.'

Bandana looked at him for an instant and said, 'Dijubabu once told me that nothing escaped his dada's eyes. I did not realize how true that was. I honestly do not want to see you unwell, but your ill health has rescued me. Escaping from them is a relief. I intend to stay here till you get well, and then head straight to my father. I'm not going back to Masi. I met those whom I was keen to meet, given my faraway life in Bombay, and now I have had enough of them. I have no wish to spend even another day in their company.'

Bipradas silently looked at Bandana while she carried on, 'All they talk about are clothes, cars, and stories of false love. I know nothing about Nainital or Mussourie, or of hotels there. But I do know that the suppressed nasty hints in their conversation were so disgusting that I wanted to run away. Sitting here now, I have the feeling that I lived my last few days in a violent tornado which spewed dust and dirt. How can they live in this kind of world?'

Bipradas said, 'That mystery is beyond me. Perhaps, they exist like graves in the desert.'

Bandana heaved a sigh, 'Theirs is a sad life. They have no peace of mind, nor are they saddled with religion. They don't believe in anything; yet, all they do is argue. But they have a store of knowledge through reading newspapers, and they know what is happening round the world. Not used to reading newspapers, I hardly followed what they were saying. When I got tired, I would escape for a breath of fresh air. But they carried on tirelessly.'

'If your father were here, he could have helped you. He could have told you about the news in the newspapers, and they could not have outsmarted you.'

Bandana smilingly agreed to it, 'True, my father has the habit of going through newspapers with a fine toothcomb. Why do we girls need to know all this?'

'Ah, what you are saying fits in with your mejdi, not you.'

Bandana protested, 'Do you believe that they are wiser than my mejdi? Not at all. Like empty vessels, they sound too much.'

'But one must be knowledgeable.'

'That is not necessary. False pride in their knowledge has made them vicious. Are they capable of loving others the way my mejdi does? No way. Do they have the devotion of my mejdi? Again, no. Have they any friends? I doubt it because of their mutual animosity. Their outward ostentation gives no clue as to how hollow they really are. And why all this showing off when on the inside, they are simply moth-eaten?'

Bipradas smiled and asked, 'What has gone wrong, Bandana, to make you so angry? Has someone cheated you by borrowing money from you?'

'Not cheated, but borrowed money.'

'How much?'

'Not a great deal, about four or five hundred.'

'Do you know the names of the borrowers?'

136

'I did, but have forgotten now,' Bandana laughed. 'How awful! I can't even imagine how anyone can ask for a loan given such a short acquaintance! They don't seem to have any shame, any hesitation. It was, as it were, a daily routine for them. How is it possible?'

Bipradas turned solemn. He said, 'Your masi's crowd has poisoned your mind, but not everyone is like them. If you look around, you may meet some others one day.'

Bandana said, 'If I do, well and good. I may revise my impression then. Those whom I met were all educated, all connected with high-ranking people. They appeared to me like characters out of stories and fiction, and in my eyes so strange and fascinating. I felt proud that perhaps the stain of backwardness attached to our women was no longer true. Sadly, this mistaken belief of mine has been shattered.'

'What mistaken belief? It is true that our women are advancing fast.'

Bandana smiled, 'I know it is true, but my point is that they are very few in number. To put them up on a pedestal and make a show of them is absurd.'

Bipradas countered, 'This is another sort of orthodoxy of yours. Abandoning one's faith can be ominous, Bandana. Be careful.'

Ignoring the remark, Bandana said, 'Away from this small but unimportant band of women, there is a vast population of women in Bengal. I have met none of them. Perhaps, they are not visible out in the open, but I have a feeling that they are part of the air which Bengalis breathe. Among them, some are weighty, while some insignificant—instances of weighty persons are my mejdi and her mother-in-law. My visit to Calcutta on this occasion has been extremely rewarding. Why are you laughing?'

'I was just thinking how grief for money can turn one into an orator! I too suffer from this failing.'

'What loss of money? That five hundred rupees?'

'I think so.'

Bandana laughed, 'I am not worried about the money. I will charge double my usual fee for looking after you. If you refuse, I will ask your mother.'

Annada came in and said, 'It is almost 8:00 p.m.—time for Bipin's food.'

Flustered, Bandana quickly said, 'Yes, Anudi, I should go. I am off, Mukhujyemashai.'

'Yes, go, but remember that if your nursing is not satisfactory, I will reduce your fees!'

'It will be flawless, dear Sir,' she said and went away, smiling.

EIGHTEEN

Bandana said, 'Your food is ready, shall I get it?'

Bipradas laughed, 'You are relentless in your efforts to make me lose my caste! But I have yet to perform my evening puja. Would you get my things ready first?'

'Would you wish me to do that?'

'Who else is here? I don't feel strong enough to walk to my mother's puja room, so I have to do my puja in this room. Let me see how well you set up my things—whether I can discover any flaws in that. Then I will decide whether you should bring my food to me or the cook should.'

Bandana was delighted. 'Condition accepted, but promise me, please, that should I actually pass the test, you will not fail me on a false pretext.'

'I promise, but why are you so keen to feed me with your own hand?'

'That I won't tell you.' And with that, she promptly left.

Bandana returned after ten minutes. She had bathed and was carrying a pot of water in her hand. She wiped a place clean for him to perform his puja with the end of her saree, arranged the puja things, and lit the incense on an incense stand. Then she fetched fresh clothes for Bipradas and a basin of water for him to wash. Bandana said, 'Sorry, I had no time to string a flower garland. This lapse will not be repeated tomorrow. You have just half an hour to perform your devotions. I will be back at 9:30 p.m.' She left after closing the door.

When Bandana returned after half an hour, Bipradas, having completed his puja, was relaxing on an easy chair.

'Did I pass or fail, Mukhujyemashai?'

'Passed, first division. You seem to have outdone my mother. Who can dare call you a pariah or say that you graduated from a pariah institution?'

'Can I bring your food now?'

'Yes, do, but before that, put away these puja things.'

'You do not have to tell me, I know that.' As she picked up the various items, she heard the clattering of shoes from outside the room. Annada entered and said, 'Bandana, your masi...'

Almost immediately, Masi and a couple of young girls came into the room. Bipradas got up and greeted them.

Masi said, 'We were told downstairs that Bipradasbabu is now well.'

'Yes, I am better.'

The two girls were shocked beyond words to find Bandana like that—with no shoes, wearing a tussore sari, her wet hair hanging loose down her back, her hands filled with puja paraphernalia—the sight was not only unfamiliar, but unthinkable. Bandana told the girls, 'Please move away from the door, I have to take these things back.'

One of the girls said, 'Oh, they can get polluted by our touch, is it?'

Bandana said yes and went out.

Very shortly, Bandana returned, still in the same clothes, and stood by Bipradas. Her aunt said, 'I am not cross because you left without telling us, but your cousin's wedding is tonight and you must be there.'

Bandana said, 'I am sorry Masi, but I cannot go.'

'What are you saying, Bandana? Prakriti will be very unhappy if you are not there.'

'Yes, I know that. Even so, I cannot go.'

Her aunt was much aggrieved and said, 'You deferred going back to Bombay because of this marriage, and that is why your father left you behind with us. Will he not be upset if he comes to know of this?'

One of the girls said, 'Besides that, Sudhirbabu is very annoyed. He did not approve of the way you left.'

Though Bandana looked at the girl, she spoke to her aunt, 'My absence will not stop Prakriti's marriage; but if I go, there will be no one to look after him.'

'But he is fine now. He ought to tell you to come with us,' Masi looked at Bipradas.

Bipradas smiled and said, 'Yes, Bandana should go, and I will tell her to. It will be wrong of her if she doesn't.'

Bandana shook her head and said, 'No, I do not think it would be wrong. Since you say so, I will go; but I will not stay back. I will return at night, and Masi must agree to this.'

'Can you not stay back even for one night?'

'No.'

'Fair enough.' Furious within, Masi left with the girls.

Bipradas said, 'Your masi is very upset. But why are you being so whimsical?'

Bandana replied, 'It is no whimsy. I know Masi is upset. I do not wish to go there, for I find everything about them most abhorrent.'

'Are you not going overboard, Bandana?'

'I can't say whether I am going overboard or not. I do indeed always question myself, but their company brings me no pleasure or peace. I recall that I had once visited a textile mill in Bombay, with its many machines and it multiple wheels which turned ceaselessly. The slightest unwariness could lead you to get caught and entangled by the wheels. Not that I don't like watching these machines, but I always do so with the uneasy feeling that it would be better to be away from them. But enough talk, I must get your food.' As she turned to leave, she noticed dirt and the scuff marks of shoes on the ground. She stopped and said, 'Sorry, Mukhujyemashai, I can't get your food now. You have to wait a little. I must get a servant to clean up this dirt.' Much amazed, Bipradas asked, 'Where did you pick up all these little details, Bandana? Who taught you?'

Bandana was a little taken aback by the question. 'I cannot remember who taught me. Perhaps, no one. I instinctively felt that these details are unavoidable in order for me to look after you. Otherwise, my work will be flawed.'

In the evening, Bandana appeared suitably groomed and dressed for the wedding. 'I am off to my cousin's marriage at Masi's insistence.'

Bipradas said, 'All my good wishes. I trust that you will soon get an opportunity to avenge your masi when you drag her from Punjab to Bombay.'

'I am not upset with Masi, but we will drag you to Bombay. Don't be alarmed. We will look after your expenses for the journey.' She then laughed and said, 'I will be late in returning, but I have made all the arrangements for your needs. If something goes awry, I will be vastly annoyed.'

'Of course, you should be, or else others will be astonished. They will think you are perhaps not well, or perhaps the food at the marriage did not agree with you.'

'Thank you, that's enough about me. Please listen to me. Do not go down for your evening prayers. Anudi will fetch everything in your room. Half an hour after that, the cook will get your food, and an hour later, Jharu will give your medicines, put out the lights, and close the door. Those are my instructions to all of them. Do you follow me?'

'Yes, I do.'

'I am off now.'

'Bye then. I must say you are looking lovely in these clothes. These clothes look natural on you, while what you wear here seems artificial.'

'What are you saying, Mukhujyemashai? They say that you do not approve of women wearing shoes.'

'They are wrong in the same way as they are when they say that I can't eat food from your hands.'

Bandana was puzzled. 'How can they be wrong? You truly had inhibitions about having food touched by me.'

'Yes, I did, but had they been genuine, they would still have persisted.'

Bandana was confused and could not comprehend the significance of what Bipradas said. Yet, she could not dismiss his words as false. She said, 'Dijubabu once told me that no one can read what is in his dada's mind; they can only go by what he says openly. What is entrenched in your heart remains acutely entrenched. Is that true?'

He just smiled and said, 'You are getting late. If you do not really wish to stay back there, then come back.'

'I will return, Mukhujyemashai. I can't stay there.' So saying, Bandana went down.

***

When they met in the morning the next day, Bipradas asked, 'So your cousin's marriage went off without a hitch, I trust?'

'Yes, there was no hitch.'

'And you stuck obstinately to your own stand. Paid no heed to Masi's request. How late was it when you returned?'

'Around 3:00 a.m. in the morning. Sadly, I could not comply with my masi's wishes. I came back late at night.' She paused, wondering if she should say what was in her mind. Then she resumed, 'I was there only for a few hours, but accomplished a great deal. I achieved in a few minutes what I had not been able to do for a year. I ended my relationship with Sudhir.'

Bipradas was jolted. 'What are you saying?'

'Yes, that is so, but I did not leave him floundering. Remember the girl you saw yesterday? Her name is Hemnalini Ray. I left Sudhir in her hands.'

Bipradas, still puzzled, asked, 'What has gone wrong? What does it mean that you ended things with Sudhir?'

Bandana said, 'I mean that it has ended. But there was nothing abrupt about it. Sudhir drew me aside and told me that what I had done was most improper. So I asked him what it was that I had done. According to him, my leaving Masi's house to come here unexpectedly without telling anybody—by which he meant not telling him—was absolutely reprehensible. Particularly because no one was there other than Bipradasbabu. I said that Annadadidi was there. Sudhir said that she was a mere servant. When I said that everyone in the house called her didi, the girl Hem said with a sly grin that she believed that was a common practice in village societies and that all it did was to add to the vanity of the servants. Sudhir told me, "You have told them that you will not stay back and must return the same night. None of us approve of your staying alone in that house. What would your father say if he comes to know about this?" I said, "What my father would think is my concern and not yours. Do you also not approve of me staying alone in that house?" The girl Hem said, "Of course, he does not; he is a part of them all." I did not want to react to this unnecessary interruption, so I turned to Sudhir and told him, "In reply to your remark, I can say that I did not like it when you took unnecessary leave and stayed back in Calcutta, but I won't. Your nasty insinuations befit people of an inferior class, but I was not aware that in a high society like yours, such conduct is also not unusual. But I have no time now, my car is waiting." The girl blurted out, "What is unseemly or improper can be discussed by any class of people, high or low." I said, "Do that to your heart's content, but I am off." Sudhir turned pale. Composing himself, he said, "Won't you even inform your masi?" I said, "I have already told her that soon after the marriage, I will leave."

'Sudhir then asked, "Can I meet you tomorrow?"

'"No," I said.

'"The next day?"

'"No."

'"When can we meet then?"

'"I cannot give you any time."

'"But I have an important matter to discuss with you."

'"You may have, but I have none."

'Sudhir did not venture to see me off to the car. He simply stood there, like a man lost.'

Bipradas smiled and said, 'This does not mean the end, Bandana. It is just a minor tiff. If you don't believe me, check with your sister.'

Bandana answered unsmilingly, 'There is no need to talk to anyone. I know it is all over between us. It cannot be revived.'

Bipradas appeared confused and said, 'Really Bandana? How can such a major relationship be terminated so easily? Do think of Sudhir's shock.'

'I have done so, but it will not take Sudhir long to get over this shock. Hem will show him the way. But I was thinking about myself. This thought occupied me in the car on my way back. I also did not sleep well last night. I admit I was uncomfortable, but felt no pain.'

'That will happen when you get over your anger. You will keep waiting until then for Sudhir to come back to you.'

Bandana said calmly, 'I am not angry; my only regret is that perhaps I should not have spoken to him so harshly when I came away. I gave him the impression that it was his fault and that I was the hurt person, which is not true. I feel mortified that I left him with such a false impression. That is all.' Her eyes moistened as she spoke.

Bipradas realized that Bandana was not pretending. He asked her, 'Do you really not love Sudhir any longer?'

'No.'

'But you did once? How could you lose it so easily?'

'It was because it was gone so easily that I found the answer equally easily. Or else, I would have been guilty of lying to you. You asked if I was really ever fond of Sudhir. Once I did believe so, then I saw someone else and Sudhir went out of my mind. But that other person has also gone out of my mind. You will probably despise me for being such a fickle-minded character. It is something shameful that no woman would like to admit, as it tarnishes her image. I could not have admitted this to anyone, but, for some reason, you seem to be an exception. I feel no inhibition in talking freely to you.'

Bipradas remained quiet, but Bandana continued, 'Perhaps, it is my nature or something to do with my age. The heart does not like to remain empty; it goes on looking everywhere. Perhaps, it is true for every woman—not everyone finds love in her life. Perhaps, it is never to be found; it is elusive like a mirage.'

Bipradas stayed silent, while Bandana went on, unchecked, 'My marriage was fixed with Sudhir a year ago, but had to be deferred due to his mother's illness. Last night, I kept wondering in my room that had the marriage gone through as planned, would I have rejected him as I did now? How could I have kept my heart in check? On grounds of decency? Tradition? But if my unruly heart rebelled, what then? Would I have taken recourse to scheming and secrecy, deceiving people with insincere smiles, as the people I spent these past few days with did? Would I be reduced to backbiting, jealousy, and animosity? Mukhujyemashai, why are you silent?'

Bipradas said, 'How can I keep pace with the storm that is raging in your heart? That is why I am quiet.'

Bandana countered, 'This won't do. You cannot get away with this. I demand a reply.'

'Unless you calm down, what is the point of my reply? Your mental state is not as it normally is, so you will not be able to follow me.'

'Why can't I? I have not lost my mind!'

'No, you have not, but you are confused. Let it be for now. When you come to me in the evening after your chores are over, more settled in your mind, then I will tell you. If I can, I will try to give you a reply then.'

'Fair enough. I also have no time now.' Bandana went out. Truly, there was no end to Bandana's work. Annada had left for Kalighat in the morning, and her responsibilities were then Bandana's. So many servants worked there, so many boys lived there and went to school and college—they all had different needs. Faced with the heavy load of work, Bandana forgot that she had had a sleepless night and that she was exhausted.

After Bipradas had had his dinner, and after completing all her chores, Bandana came to his room. She asked, 'Mukhujyemashai, will you give me a truthful answer if I ask you something?'

Bipradas said, 'I normally do, but what is your question?'

Bandana asked, 'Tell me, do you really love Mejdi? You were married when both of you were very young—many years ago—was there never any deviation?'

Bipradas was struck dumb. It was beyond his imagination that such a thought could occur to anyone. After collecting himself, he replied, 'Better ask your mejdi.'

Bandana remarked, 'But how should she know? Nobody ever has a clue about your innermost thoughts. I will figure it out one way or another. But if you do tell me, let it be the truth.'

'I will tell you the truth, but do you not trust me?'

'Not always. I know you are a great man, but still only a man. I get the impression somehow that you are very lonely and have no companion. Is this not true?'

Bipradas skirted the issue and said, 'To love my wife is my moral duty.'

Bandana observed, 'You are faultless within the ambit of your moral code, but is there nothing beyond that in this world?'

'Not that I can see.'

Bandana said, 'But I can. Shall I tell you?'

Bipradas's face paled. With outstretched hands, he said, 'No, not another word. Go back to your room now. Tomorrow or day after, when you are back to your senses, I will give you my answer. Or maybe, you will find the answer on your own. Those who clouded your mind in your masi's house cannot have the last word. Those who stick to their moral code also have their place in this world. No, no more arguments. Leave me now.'

Bandana knew that that order could not be ignored. Perhaps, it was that very element which intimidated everyone. Silently, Bandana left the room.

NINETEEN

The next evening, Bandana told Bipradas, 'I am going back once again to my masi's place. This time not for an hour, but until Masi can arrange for someone to take me back to Bombay.'

'What do you mean?'

'It means that an urgent telegram carrying Father's instructions has arrived. Masi will send her car tomorrow morning to take me back.'

Bipradas said, 'It is clear that your masi has both the patience and the intelligence to take her revenge. This telegram is probably a reply to her telegram. May I have a look at it?'

'No. I cannot show it to you.'

Bipradas was silent and then said with a little laugh, 'This is a grand instance of God taking measure of one's vanity. I had always believed that nobody can get me entangled into anything, but I was wrong. Apparently, there are people who can do so like your masi. Let me at least read the telegram to see how serious the accusations against me are.'

Bandana then let him see the telegram. It was a long message from Raysahib. Bipradas read the entire content and gave it back. He said, 'On the whole, there is nothing unfair in what your father said. There is a risk attached to selfless good work, nor is it an easy task to look after sick relations.'

Bandana asked, 'Are you suggesting that I go back to my masi?'

'Bandana, it is your father's wish. It is not the home of Mukhujyes of Balarampur, so your Mukhujyemashai has no role here. Masi has contrived to convey this instruction via your father, so there is no way you can disobey it.'

'But these words of yours are very trite. My father has no clue about anything; yet I have to follow this instruction, whether it is fair or not. You know the kind of house my masi has.'

Bipradas said, 'Not quite. But from what you told me, it is not a very congenial place. If I were well, I would have accompanied you to Bombay, but sadly I am still not strong enough.'

'How can I leave you in this condition? Must the wishes of a masi whom I hardly know prevail?'

'What else can you do?'

'Not go there at all.'

'Well, then stay back. But send a telegram to your father. What will you tell Masi when she comes to fetch you?'

'I will tell her that I can't go. Just that, no more.'

'Your masi may not just stop there. She might send a telegram to my mother.'

That had not occurred to Bandana. It set her thinking. She said, 'You may be right. Perhaps, it has already been done. Do you know why?'

Bipradas said, 'It is not possible to know, but my guess is that all this effort is not entirely free of self-interest, nor is it for your sole benefit. Perhaps, she has a motive of her own.'

Bandana said, 'And I know what it is. A nephew of hers has qualified as a barrister. And she has already introduced us. It is her firm belief that he is the most befitting mate for me. And the motive? I am my father's only child, and the money he will leave behind will comfortably see him through even if he does not earn a penny.'

Bipradas said, 'It is not unusual for an aunt to be concerned about a nephew. How is he in looks?'

'Fine.'

'Like me?'

Bandana laughed, 'You are being vain now. You know it very well that there is no one in the world comparable to you in looks, and if one takes that into account, then most girls will have to remain spinsters. They will keep waiting for you hopelessly. Ashok is a decent-looking person, and I ought not to be too finicky.'

'So may I take it that you like him?'

'Well, no one can fault me if I do.' Bandana then got up and said, 'Almost 5:00 p.m.—time for your barley water. Let me get it. Meanwhile, give some thought to Ashok.' She returned five minutes later, carrying a silver glass of barley water chilled with ice and, as she squeezed lemon juice into it, she said, 'Now drink up the whole glass. You can't leave even a drop. I will not accept it if people seek to blame me for not being attentive enough.'

Bipradas said, 'I see that you have fully mastered the art of coercion, so nobody can double-cross you.'

When Bipradas finished his barley water, Bandana picked up the empty glass. As she was about to go, she turned back and asked, 'Can you tell me who loves you the most in this world?'

'I can.'

'Will you tell me who?'

'Bandana Devi.'

Bandana fled. But she returned after about fifteen minutes, drew up a chair close to the bed, and sat down. Bipradas asked with a smile, 'Why did you rush away like that?'

Bandana was first lost for words, and then spoke softly, 'I simply couldn't bear to hear the words. I had the unpleasant feeling that I had been caught red-handed while thieving.'

'Is that why you cannot look straight at me?'

'Of course, I can.' And then she forced herself to raise her face. She tried to laugh it away, but almost immediately, her face went red. After she was able to control herself, she asked, 'How did you know?'

Bipradas replied, 'A superfluous question. Do you think that I am so stony-hearted that I am incapable of comprehending even this much? Besides, even if I had any doubt, it disappeared when I looked at your face.'

Bandana lowered her face again. Bipradas told her, 'No, Bandana, no. This won't do. Look up. You have nothing to be ashamed of, particularly not with me. Look up and listen to me.'

It was the same old commanding voice. Bandana looked up and said, 'You must be furious with me.'

154

Bipradas responded, 'No, not the least. Is this something to be furious about about? But I hope that some day you will discover your error, and it is only then that you will find the remedy.'

'But what if I never discover my error? In fact, what if I never see it as a mistake at all?'

'You will, Bandana, you will. If you have no idea how such affairs lead to tragedies, then I will not accept that you have really loved me. It has been nothing but a passing whim of yours like your love for Sudhir. Just to distract yourself by thinking that you have someone close to your heart. No more than that.'

Bandana was greatly upset. She spoke in a hurt voice, 'Please don't compare yourself to Sudhir. It is thoroughly unacceptable. I do accept that it may spawn many mishaps and lead to many tragedies, but I will not admit that it is unreal. If it was, could I have received any love from you? Have I not received any?'

Bipradas was listening to Bandana attentively. He assured her, 'You have, Bandana, you have indeed. How else could I have eaten food served by you? What could have motivated me to accept your care day and night? But granting all that, does that mean I should sink into a profane world and drag you down with me? There are those who are able to stand with their heads held high because of their faith in me. Must I shatter them and let them down? Are you asking me to do that?'

Bandana said firmly, 'You have to then declare that what you are unable to sacrifice now is your vanity. Admit truthfully

155

that the desire to be considered great takes precedence. Or else, why this sense of shame? What do we accept as evil? This man-made code that men have followed time and again and equally violated time and again? You may be able to do it, but I cannot.'

Bipradas said gravely, 'You may not, but I can, and that would serve us fine. You have read a lot of literature in English, and equally learnt a great deal at your masi's home. It will take time for you to get over all that.'

Bandana said, 'You're making fun of me again, but believe me, I am pretty serious.'

'I follow you, but who put this craziness in your head?'

'You did.'

'I? Am I the source of your misguided notions?'

'Yes, who else? Perhaps not deliberately, but it is you, nevertheless.'

Bipradas looked at her speechlessly. Bandana continued, 'What you criticize as evil is not acceptable to me. I also believe that what you accept as righteous is nothing but a sort of prejudice—it may be firmly held—but that is what is is.'

'You may be right, Bandana,' Bipradas said, inclining his head in agreement. 'It may be prejudice, but it is a firm prejudice. Believe me, when a person's religious faith takes the form of this prejudice, it is then that faith becomes real and simple. There are no conflicts in your life, so you do not have to resist them. You are at peace with yourself. Perhaps, this is what I label as Bipradas's unshakeable faith.'

'Will it never change, Mukhujyemashai?'

'That is what I believe, Bandana. I cannot conceive even now how it can change.'

Bandana's eyes filled with tears. Bipradas tenderly took her hands in his and said, 'But why do we need any change? I do love you, and that love is deeply entrenched in my heart. From now on, this love will give me comfort when I am in trouble; it will sustain me when I am frail; and when I cannot carry on with my life all by myself, I will remember you. Will you then come to me?'

Bandana dried her eyes and said, 'I will if I have the strength to do so, and if I am free to come, not otherwise.'

Bipradas was taken aback. 'True, very true, only if you are free. I hope that road is never blocked. Do come then, don't sulk and turn away from me.'

Bandana once again wiped her eyes and said, 'I have but one request of you. Don't speak of this to anyone.'

'No, I won't, but you know that I have no one to talk to.'

'Yes, I know.'

They both remained quiet for sometime.

Bipradas asked, 'How did you guess that I am so lonely in this vast world?'

Bandana answered, 'Honestly, I do not know how. That day when I left your house in a bad mood, you came along with us. Can you recall those drunken Anglo-Indians in the train? It was not a big matter, and yet I felt that you were different from those around us. Nothing stops you from taking the sole responsibility for everything. Dijubabu had once told me that. I found also that you expect nothing from anyone. That night in bed, I kept thinking about you. Sleep eluded me. Early in the morning, I saw a light in the puja room and found you meditating. I kept gazing at you when I suddenly realized that it was nearly dawn and the servants would be up. To avoid being seen, I quietly returned to my room. But I have never gotten over that image of you—even now I see it when I close my eyes.'

Bipradas laughed, 'Did you really see me doing puja?'

Bandana said, 'I have also seen your mother doing puja, but it was not the same thing. It is vastly different. What do you meditate upon, Mukhujyemashai?'

Bipradas asked, 'What will you gain by this knowledge? You are not going to practise it.'

'No, I will not. Still, I am curious.'

Bipradas said nothing. Bandana resumed, 'That very day, it became clear to me that even in a crowd, you are different; you stand alone. No one can attain the level at which they could give you company. Can I ask you something else?'

'What is it, Bandana?'

'Perhaps, you do not need the love of a woman—right?'

'What do you mean?'

'Truthfully, I do not know. I just thought of asking you. It is likely that you no longer have such desires. It is all trivial to you now. Is that not so?'

Bipradas just smiled.

The sound of a car was heard, and Dwijadas's voice too. Annada came in and announced the arrival of Dwijadas.

'Is he alone or did someone come with him?'

'He is alone.'

Bandana stood up and said, 'Let me go and see to his food.'

When Dwijadas came the next day at morning and touched Bipradas's feet, he noticed Bandana setting up the things for his puja in a corner. Dwijadas said, 'The inaugaration of Ma's pond is scheduled for the next fifth day of the moon. It's going to be a massive affair, Dada.'

'All events of Ma's are usually done on a massive scale. What is the problem?'

Dwijadas said, 'That is true, but combined with this is the prayer service she vowed to have if Basu recovered. That by itself is not a small do. From the list of payments to be made to high priests and the relatives expected to attend that I learned from Boudie, I fear that this mission will account for a substantial dent in your funds. So, be forewarned!'

Bandana burst into laughter when she heard it. Other than Mother, no one let pass the opportunity to malign Bipradas as a miser. Bipradas joined in the laughter and told Dwijadas, 'But it is your turn now to provide the funds.'

'Mine? All right, I agree. But that will call for some change in plans. The priests who will preside will not be from tols, rather those who have been kept locked out.'

'Why are you so anti-tol? You have just heard about them from unsubstantiated verbal reports, without knowing anything about them personally. In your governance, I may have to possibly starve, as I am one of them.'

Dwijadas promptly touched his dada's feet again and said, 'Never say that. You do not belong to either of these groups, though I do not know of any third group. All that I have ever known is that Dada is beyond our comprehension.'

Deflecting the conversation, Bipradas asked, 'I trust that the news of my illness has not reached Ma's ears?'

'No, but it would have been better to have done so, for it would have effectively stopped this hullabaloo about the new pond.'

'Have arrangements been made to fetch the relatives?'

'The process is on. From the past, the present, and the future—everybody. Akshaybabu has been invited along with his daughter. Ma believes that the participation in this great event will be Maitreyee's ordeal by fire. I have been charged with the job of escorting them.'

'Has Ma talked about anyone else to be taken there?'

'Yes, Anudi and any of the college boys if they want to.'

'No request from your boudie?'

'No, none.'

The sound of another car was heard. Bandana looked out and saw that it was her masi. She left the room.

'Let me go and have a wash,' Dwijadas said and left. Bipradas performed his puja, but it was Annada who fetched his food. She told him that Bandana was occupied with the girl who had come to take her.

Dwijadas returned, carrying a long list of items he had to procure and arrange to dispatch to Balarampur. While the two brothers were deeply engrossed in that affair, Bandana spoke from outside the room, 'Mukhujyemashai, may I come in please? But I have my shoes on.'

'It does not matter. Do come in.'

Bandana came in. She was wearing the same clothes in which she was first seen at Balarampur. Much surprised, Bipradas asked, 'Are you off somewhere?'

'Yes, to my masi's.'

'When will you be back?'

'I do not know.' She bowed low, but did not touch his feet. Without lifting her head, she greeted Dwijadas and left.

TWENTY

Dwijadas asked, 'Why did Bandana leave so suddenly? Is it because of me?'

Bipradas said, 'No, her father has sent a telegram asking her to stay with her masi until she returns to Bombay.'

'How did a masi surface? Bandana hardly spoke to me. True, she did greet me when she left, but her face was turned away. What has she got against me?'

Bipradas did not give a reply, but explained to him about Masi. He told Dwijadas, 'Anudi was nervous because of my illness and fetched Bandana from her masi's home to look after me. She did a great job. You should all be grateful to her.'

Dwijadas said, 'Granted, but it was a rare fortune to have the opportunity to nurse you. If she has really appreciated how precious this opportunity had been for her, then she should be grateful to us.'

Bipradas smiled and said, 'You are a terrible person.'

Dwijadas said, 'Terrible I may be, but I am not a fool. If a report of her devoted service to you reaches Mother's ears, Mother will be indebted to her forever. Not a minor gain, is it?'

'Ah, so have you finally come to appreciate Ma after such a long time?'

'If I have, then let that knowledge remain with you. Let Ma persist in her belief that I am a wicked son, a black sheep of the family. No need to dispel that belief.'

'But why? Are you saying that you truly do not wish Ma to trust you, to think well of you? What do gain by this attitude?'

'Perhaps nothing, but neither am I desirous of it. I have earned your affection and received Boudie's unstinting love— that is my king's ransom which I could never exhaust even if I generously gave it away over seven generations. What more do I need?' As he said it, his face turned crimson with embarrassment. Always a withdrawn person, he rarely allowed his emotions to take over. All his life, it had been his nature to keep his emotions hidden under a guise of indifference. He quickly recovered and said, 'All this talk is pointless. Bandana's abrupt departure looked to me to be a sign of her displeasure. Can you explain this to me?'

'It may mean this. Having seen you, she felt that may be she was no longer needed. The task of looking after me now devolves on you.' Saying that, Bipradas started laughing.

Dwijadas said, 'I know you are saying this in jest, but let me tell you that there will come a day when these English-educated girls will sink in their own vanity. I sincerely hope that I will never see the day when I will need to look after my sick dada, but if I have to, it will not take me time to prove that ten Bandanas cannot measure up to Diju's service to Dada. Please pass this message on to Bandana.'

Bipradas's face glowed with love. He said, 'Yes, I will, but I do not know if she will believe me. You do not have to pass this test for your dada, but for the sake of only one person—Ma. Both of you need to come to an understanding. Do you follow me, Diju?'

Dwijadas said, 'No, not quite. As she is my mother and still with us, then one day or another, we will need to come to an understanding, but I do not follow why there is a pressing need for that now. It is just my fate; everything in my life is topsy-turvy. My father left me nothing, but you gave me what I have. My mother gave me birth, but it was Anudi who raised me, and it was under the care of Boudie that I grew up—both of them being outsiders. Tell me, Dada, how long can I carry on reciting the age-old litany of hymns of praise to my parents?'

Bipradas said, 'I will not at the moment take up my mother's defence. You will come to know the truth yourself. But your impression about Father is wholly wrong. You are very truly the owner of half the estate left by him.'

Dwijadas said, 'You may be right. But after Father's death, did you not burn his will and testament behind locked doors?'

'Who told you this?'

'Directly from her who has protected me in every way.'

'That may be, but your boudie never read that will. It is possible that Father willed everything to you, and out of frustration I destroyed that will. That is not impossible.'

Highly amused, Dwijadas began to laugh and said, 'I thought you never lied. In the age of Dwapar, Vedavyas made a note of Yudhisthir's lie, and in the present age of Kali, I will make a note of your lie. Let us not add more to our sins. Just tell me what is it that you wish me to do.'

'You will have to take charge of our property, assets, and business affairs.'

'But why? Please tell me why must I assume all this responsibility? Is it that you cannot cope with all this by yourself? That is not possible. Is it because I am becoming lazy and useless? No, I am not. Tell Ma that I have no need for material wealth. I will continue to be worthless. But I will not take charge of our property and our money while you are still here. Must I, in the end, become a deeply involved man of property? People will start saying that blood does not flow through my veins. What flows is a stream of money.' Dwijadas noticed that Bipradas was not paying any attention to his words, which was unusual for him. Somewhat perturbed, he asked, 'Dada, do you really wish me to take charge of the estate and sacrifice my long-standing dream of dedicating my life to the cause of our country's freedom?'

'I have never stopped you. Let your dream remain with you forever—even so, I ask you to take charge of the family.'

'Tell me why? Unless I have an answer to this, I will not accept this obligation.'

'Surely, the reason is quite clear. I am here today, but it can so happen that I am no longer here.'

Dwijadas said forcefully, 'No, this cannot happen. That is beyond my conception.'

The intensity of his faith bothered Bipradas, yet he smiled and said, 'Nothing is impossible in this world. Those who refuse to see this only deceive themselves. It could also be that I feel exhausted and need some rest. Would you deny me even that?'

'No, Dada, I cannot deny you that. Just tell me what is it that I have to do and from when.'

'From today.'

'So soon? Fair enough, Dada. I cannot disobey you.' He left, but as he went out, he heard his dada say, 'You don't have to tell me this. You never disobey me.'

Dwijadas embarked on his duties immediately. All his life, he was used to being maligned as idle, useless, and indifferent, but it did not take him long to dispel his poor reputation when he was put in charge of ensuring the success of his mother's mission. Bipradas hardly expected that Dwijadas, unused as he was, would be able to carry out such a major assignment with such ease. His untiring, well-disciplined labour and competency in the discharge of his work caught Bipradas by surprise. Whatever needed to be procured and dispatched to Balarampur was done. He assembled relatives and family connections together and saw them off with appropriate honour. When he went to see Bipradas for further instructions before returning home, he found Bandana in his brother's room. Her presence puzzled him and, after a formal greeting, he said, 'Dada, I am catching tonight's train to go home, and Akshaybabu, his wife, and their daughter Maitreyee are travelling with me. Your college students will probably travel tomorrow or the day after. I have paid their rail fares. You have to take Anudi with you. Please see that you are not late.'

'Do I have to go?'

'Yes, I believe so. If you don't go, please get a pair of wooden sandals which I will place on the throne, as Bharat did in Rama's absence.'

Bipradas laughed, 'Must you be flippant? I really wonder about Akshaybabu. How can he go now? His college is not closed. Is he going to skip college?'

Dwijadas said, 'Most likely. But he has nothing to lose. It is far more important for him to get his daughter married off into a rich family. An affluent son-in-law means a great deal for the future. Much better than the fixed salary of a college.'

A much-riled Bipradas said, 'Your words are as crude as they are harsh. Can you not speak with due respect about a person?'

Dwijadas said, 'Better check with Boudie if I can or not. My problem is I do not unnecessarily overuse my sense of decorum.'

Bipradas could not resist breaking out in laughter. 'For everything, you have your solitary witness—your boudie. Like a wine vendor standing in witness for a drunk.'

Dwijadas said, 'Perhaps. But your words are not exactly melodic. I am not a drunkard, nether is she a purveyor of alcohol. On the contrary, what she provides is nectar, and privately she feeds a host of needy people which many wealthy persons do not.'

Bipradas retaliated, 'Of course, they do not because they have lots more to do than creating a beast out of her brother-in-law through sheer indulgence.'

Bandana started giggling, although keeping her head down, which did not escape Dwijadas. He said, 'I have no wish to get into an argument about this issue. You do not have a boudie of your own, so you have no idea about what a boudie's love is in a Bengali home. It is useless to expound on this. I see that Bandana is amused, but instead of living with her masi, if she could come and stay at our place, she might appreciate my point. But enough talk. Just tell me, when do you plan to go home?'

'I am very fatigued. Can you not explain this to Ma?'

Bipradas's voice had never sounded so lifeless and dispirited to Dwijadas. It did not seem like his dada was speaking. Pained and anguished, he asked, 'Are you still unwell, Dada?'

'No, I am fine now.'

'Then how do I explain to Ma that you won't be going to her function? She will be scared and come running here, abandoning her unfinished job. All her arrangements will go for a toss.'

Bipradas asked, 'When do you propose I go there?'

Dwijadas said, 'Today, tomorrow, the day after, whenever. If you allow me, I will come and take you with me.'

Bipradas said, 'Okay, but you do not have to come back. I can manage to travel on my own.'

After Dwijadas left, Bandana asked, 'Why are you unwilling to go home, Mukhujyemashai?'

Bipradas said, 'You heard my reason.'

'Yes, but those excuses are for others, not for me. You must tell me the truth.'

'I feel exhausted.'

'No.'

'Why not? Fatigue overtakes everyone, why not me?'

'Fatigue can also affect you. But if it were genuine in your case, I would have been the first person to detect this. You can deceive others, but not me. Before I go, I will leave a note for Mejdi that should she ever need to get to the bottom of your ailment, she can call me.'

'Your mejdi cannot fathom my ailment, but you can—she won't be pleased to be told so.'

'True, she will not be pleased. But she will be grateful to me. My mejdi belongs to the times when she did not have to select her husband. He came to her like a gift from God and, since then, she has always found him fit and strong. How would she know that there may come a time when he would pass through a mental depression?'

Bipradas smiled and remained quiet. Bandana asked, 'Why do you smile?'

Bipradas replied, 'My smile comes naturally. It is beyond your conception that there could be people who fall outside your circle of those who have been on the lookout for husbands. You are confined to your own familiar world and do not recognize the exceptions. Yet, these exceptions are what sustain our religious beliefs, our concept of virtue, our literature, and our unshakeable faith and respect. Otherwise, the whole world would have been reduced to an arid desert. You have not grasped this truth even now.'

Mockingly, Bandana said, 'I suppose that you are this exception yourself. But did you not tell me the other day that you love me as well?'

'I still maintain that, but your idea of love is one-dimensional; there is no other. And that is why you did not fully grasp the significance of my words to you. Just go and have look at Diju and his boudie. If you are not blind, you will see for yourself how love and regard have intermingled. In their fun and jokes, in their fondness and happiness, in their deep intimacy, she is just not his boudie—she is his friend, she is his mother. This is precisely the bond between you and me. How could you not accept me like that?'

His voice was sort of a mixture of tenderness and admonition, which rankled Bandana. She kept quiet for a while and then suddenly said, 'I did misunderstand you. I would not be unhappy if you really loved Mejdi, but you do not. All you know is your code of conduct and your duty, and you strictly follow that. You are a hard person by nature, so you do not know how to love. One day this truth will be known, regardless of your desire to suppress it.'

She lapsed into silence for some time and then resumed, 'I too have realized my mistake today. Please let me have your blessings so that I no longer continue to search for my man in this vast empty universe.'

With a smile, Bipradas extended his arm and said, 'Yes, I can do that. Let there be an end today to your search for a man. God will gift you the man who will be forever yours.'

Bandana took that remark as an insult and responded, 'You are making a mistake, Mukhujyemashai. Searching for a man is not my calling. Others may do it. But I have not yet told you what brings me back today. An erroneous belief of mine has been dispelled. While I was staying here, I started to believe that all your customs and manners must be good—observing the rigours of pollution by touch, making sandalwood paste, arranging for puja requirements, and such other details—I thought that all these things truly sanctified people. I realized my foolishness back at my masi's house. For a few days of insanity, I believed that all your rites and rituals were right, accepting that they were not different from our education and beliefs.' She broke into a loud laughter.

She expected that what she said would wound Bipradas, but it was not so. With a pleasant smile, he said, 'I knew this, Bandana. Can you recall that on the first day, I had cautioned you that this was not for you, so you better not fall for it? I am happy that you have seen through your errors. You thought that this would hurt me, but that is not true. It never upsets me if someone does not do something that is contrary to one's nature. You once asked me what the subject of my meditation was. I did not give you an answer then, not because there was a barrier, but because it was unnecessary. Anyway, let us end this conversation. Tell me, has a date been fixed for your return to Bombay?'

Bandana was deeply hurt and said, 'No.'

'The other day you told me of your masi's nephew, Ashok. You also said that you thought well of the young man. Any further developments there?'

'None.'

'You will have my blessings if you two get married, but one word of caution. Do not do anything under pressure from your masi. Be careful.'

'I will.'

Bipradas said, 'I am going home tomorrow or the day after. I will be back soon. If you are still in Calcutta, do come and see me.'

What Bandana said with a shake of her head was not all that clear.

Bipradas said, 'You may have heard that my leave from family responsibilities has been sanctioned. My father put me in charge when I was very young. I never had any free time to go anywhere. I now feel a great sense of relief.'

Bandana asked, 'Do you really need this relief? Are you indeed so exhausted?'

Bipradas evaded a direct answer to that question, and instead said, 'I told them about how wonderfully you looked after me when I was unwell, and also told them that they should be grateful to you, as they could not have done even half of what you did. Diju admitted this gratitude, but at the same time asked me to remind you that if ever the situation arose, not even ten Bandanas could match his efforts.'

Bandana said, 'Please tell him that I accept this challenge. If the occasion for such a test does arise, I trust he will be there.'

'He will be there, Bandana, he will. He is not the kind to back out. You don't really know him.'

'Yes, Mukhujyemashai, I know. I know it well. No Bandana can ever match him when it comes to look after you.'

A sense of pride for his brother lit up Bipradas's face. He said, 'Do you know that my Diju is a very saintly person?'

'More than you?'

'Yes, more than me.' For a moment, he was distracted. Then he said, 'He says you are very annoyed with him. Why did you not speak to him?'

'There was no need for me to do so.'

'You are indeed cross with him. Let me tell you something. Diju's conduct may sometimes appear rough. What he says is always not so gentle, but if you ever see him without his disguise, you will find no sweeter person than him. Do believe what I just told you. Nor will you easily find such a reliable soul.'

Bandana appeared cool. She just stood up and said, 'My car has been waiting for a long time. If I stay on, I will come and see you when you are back. Otherwise, this is my last pranam to you.' She bowed low and touched his feet and left quickly.

Crossing the verandah, she found Dwijadas standing with folded hands.

She laughed and asked, 'What does this mean?'

'Just an appeal to you. I need to take you along with Dada to our home.'

'But why?'

'That is why I am here, just to tell you that. Once, without any invitation, you stepped into our home. Would you please graciously repeat that visit?'

Bandana wavered for an instant and asked, 'But on whose invitation? Ma's, Dada's, or yours?'

'Well, in this instance, mine.'

'Do you have the authority to invite me?'

Dwijadas said, 'I may not have the right, but I do have the right to live and it is from that right I am making this appeal to you. Please say that you will. Normally, I do not ask for a favour unless I direly need it.'

Bandana took time to answer. 'Fair enough, I will go, but it will be your responsibility to protect my self-respect.'

Gratified by her acceptance, Dwijadas replied, 'Despite my limited authority, I accept that resonsibility.'

Bandana said, 'Please make sure that you do not forget it in a critical situation.'

'I shall not.'

TWENTY-ONE

Bipradas went down to his office after a gap of many days. The table was loaded with piles of papers, pending arrears from unattended work. He felt weary, but the work could no longer be neglected. It was not possible to unload the work on Diju. He was examining an accounts book when he heard a car horn, followed almost immediately by Bandana. But she was not alone. Along with her was an unknown young man dressed like an upper-class Bengali gentleman. He appeared to be under thirty years of age, and could be considered good-looking had he been a little taller. Bipradas stood up to welcome them.

Bandana said, 'Let me introduce him. This is Mr Chow-de-rey, bar-at-law. But he will not take offence if you call him Ashokbabu. I agreed to bring him here under that condition. But first let me do my duty.' Stepping up to him, she bowed her head and said, 'Sorry, in his presence, I cannot touch your feet, in case he thinks I am a disgrace to their society. For heaven's sake, do not conclude that my present action has anything to do with my masi. I happen to know what you think of her.'

Bipradas asked, 'Is that how you speak to your masi about me?' Turning to the stranger, he said, 'I have heard so much about you from Bandana. I would have gone to meet you had I not been unwell. It is good that she brought you here.'

The visitor was about to say something, but before he could do so, Bandana raised her admonitory index finger and said, 'Mukhujyemashai, you exaggerate almost to the point of a lie. Please don't overdo it.'

'What do you mean?'

'Just this that you are not different from us mortal persons. Like common people, you also make up your own stories, mixing truth with lies.'

Bipradas protested, 'Never. Ask anyone, and they will all confirm that you are impugning my character!'

Bandana said, 'In which case I will take you to them, whisk away your lion's garb, and unmask the real you. With the end of your terrifying image and freed from fear, people will rush to extol and bless me.'

Bipradas said, 'Great, no problem with the blessings. In fact, I am also prepared to join them, but you do not believe in blessings. According to you, blessings are nothing but superstition. Pointless words.'

Bandana raised her finger once again, 'What? Poking at me again? Whoever told you that we do not need blessings from our elders? That we regard them as superstitious? You are upsetting me now.'

'Am I really? Let us then say no more. But what brings you here this morning? Have you anything to do here?'

Bandana said, 'Lots. First I need an explanation from you. Why are you down here and working without my permission?'

'I am not doing anything really. I was just contemplating the possibility of working.' He pushed aside the ledger through which he had been looking.

Bandana said pleasantly, 'Explanation satisfactory, disobedience forgiven. Such devotion in future will do. Listen to me now, please. Talk to your visitor. Tell him about the magnificence of Mukhujye wealth, the thrilling tales of your reign over your tenants, and whatever else you wish to tell him. Meanwhile, I will go to Anudi and ask her to do the packing. We are going to Balarampur tomorrow by the morning train. Travelling by the day will protect us from catching cold. Mr Chow-de-rey wishes to come with me. He has never seen a large event in an affluent home with all the show and grandeur that goes with it. How could he?'

Bipradas asked, 'You must have seen many, I presume?'

Bandana replied, 'This remark is both irrelevant and impolite. I merely mentioned that he has had no such exposure. Anyway, he is so pleased that I agreed to take him to Balarampur that he will escort me later to Bombay.'

Very solemnly, Bipradas said, 'Indeed? Such self-sacrifice is rare amongst us. It can clearly be found only in your community. I am impressed.'

Bandana said, 'So you ought to be. Do I perceive a trace of envy?' As she was about to leave after levelling a strong glance of displeasure at him, Bipradas called her back and observed, 'Sounds like the fable of the dog guarding a mound of straw.

Neither can he eat it, nor will he allow the bulls to graze on it. That being so, how can men survive?'

Bandana spoke with a mock rage, 'Just like common people like us do—no difference. Men die of false fear.'

'In that case, go and rid them of this fear.'

'That is what I intend to do. And, at the same time, will avenge myself of the ill-conceived analogy with straw.' Saying that, she hurriedly left.

Bipradas turned to the visitor, 'Mr...'

Ashok modestly stopped him, 'No, that will not do. I have deliberately dressed like a Bengali just to avoid that. She also assured me that...'

It pleased Bipradas. He said, 'That is great, Ashokbabu. Addressing you is now easier. Being a rustic, I cannot always remember, nor am I used to it; but now I can talk to you in a more relaxed manner. I am told that you wish to visit our village. If you do so, I will be truly gratified. The head of our family is our mother and, on her behalf, I have the pleasure of inviting you.'

Ashok was delighted to no end by that cordial invitation. He said, 'Yes, I will come. Thank you for your kind invitation. I will have the opportunity of seeing countless numbers of poor and needy attending the ceremony, a host of scholars presiding over the event, festivities, and feasts, people coming and going—so many interesting features.'

'Bandana has apparently sketched an embroidered picture of us just for fun.'

'But why should she do that? What does she gain by that?'

'Her first gain is to put us down. She is annoyed with us. And the second gain is the ruse to persuade you to escort her to Bombay.'

Ashok said, 'It has been already agreed that if the need arises, I will escort her to Bombay. But I do not believe that she is upset with the Mukhujyes, or that she wants to put you down. Until yesterday, there was no talk of any visit to Balarampur. She and her masi had a tiff while talking about you and your family. Masi had commented, "It is praiseworthy of Bipradas's mother to excavate a new pond for the benefit of the public, but to launch it ceremonially is absolutely meaningless— nothing but a superstition. And to participate in a superstitious event, in my view, is improper." Bandana said, "They are a wealthy family and events at their home are usually observed with some show and pomp. What is so strange about it?" To which my aunt said, "I know that squandering money by rich people is not uncommon. Nevertheless, it is still a superstition. So I object to you going there." Bandana said, "I do not agree with you. On the contrary, when I try to evaluate something about which I know nothing or have never even attempted to know, I regard it as superstitious." My aunt became furious and asked, "Have you taken your father's permission?"

'Bandana replied, "I know that my father will not stop me. Besides, my didi's husband is unwell and I have been given the task of escorting him."

'"May I know who gave you this responsibility? I presume he did himself, did he not?" That question irritated Bandana so much that I feared she would have a rush of blood to her head, which might lead her to blurt out anything that came to her mind. Fortunately, she calmed down and replied quietly, "I am not used to answering any odd question that people pointlessly ask me. All I wish to tell you is that the day after tomorrow, I will travel to Balarampur taking Mukhujyemashai with me, and that is that."

'My aunt, still very angry, left. I asked, "Will you take me with you? I am very keen to see the rituals which I had never done." Bandana said, "Those are a bundle of superstitions, and you may lose your caste just watching them." I replied, "If you do not lose your caste, neither will I. Or, we may both lose our caste which, then, is not a loss to me."

'Bandana insisted, "Since you do not believe in such practices, you will just laugh quietly."

'So I asked her, "Do you believe in them?" She said, "No, I do not, but Mukhujyemashai does. I just keep hoping that his belief becomes mine one day." Bipradasbabu, deep in her heart, Bandana worships you. In fact, there is no one for whom she has such high regard.'

It was nothing new or unknown to Bipradas; but that coming from a stranger shook him.

'There was some talk of you two getting married. Has Bandana given her consent?'

'No, not yet, but neither has she said no.'

'That sounds hopeful, Ashokbabu. Saying nothing often denotes consent.'

Ashok looked gratefully at Bipradas and said, 'This may not be so, at least that is what I feel. My main problem is that

I am poor, and she is rich. It is not that I am indifferent to money, but unlike my aunt, that is not my sole object. How can I explain to her that I am not a party to my aunt's plan?'

Until then, Bipradas had been cool towards him, but the simplicity of his words stemmed that feeling. He said kindly, 'It will take no time for Bandana to understand that you do not subscribe to your aunt's plan, if it be true. Following that, it will also take no time for her to be favourably disposed towards you. The issue of money will not be an impediment.'

'Are you positive, Bipradasbabu?' Ashok asked anxiously.

Bipradas hesitated in answering him. He wavered and paused, and then said, 'I infer this from what little I know of her.'

Ashok said, 'But do you know what I really need? It is your favourable disposition rather than hers. And the day I have that, there will be nothing more for me to ask for.'

Bipradas smiled and asked, 'Who put this bizarre idea into your head that it is my favourable disposition that will influence her choice of husband? Surely, not Bandana herself? If she did, that must be in jest.'

'No, not in jest, that is the truth.'

'And who told you?'

Ashok replied, 'It is not something that someone has to say, Bipradasbabu. After her fight with her masi, Bandana unexpectedly came to my room—which was very unusual—and said, "You have to take me to Bombay." I said, "Whenever you say." Then she said, "I am leaving for Balarampur and will tell you in due time." I told her, "Fine, but why did you so infuriate your masi? You do not really believe in their pujas, their scriptures, their sacrifices and prayers, or their deities, but you still asserted that you would feel relieved if you could truly believe in all that. Why did you say that?" She said, "What I said was not untrue. If I could accept all that in genuine belief like them, I would feel truly blessed. I looked after Mukhujyemashai when he was unwell. And, in return, I will ask for a boon from him, praying for that faith." She kept talking about you. It was beyond my imagination that a person could be so devoted to someone that one could be this absorbed in praying for the good of that somebody. She spoke about an episode while talking about you. She used to arrange your puja things during your illness. One morning, she was rather late and, when she came out in a hurry, her foot struck something. As much as she tried to assure herself that it would not cause any hindrance to your devotions, she could not convince herself that it would be so. So, she went for a fresh bath and rearranged the puja things. You were displeased that day and told her, "Bandana, if you cannot get up in the morning, leave it to Anudi to take care of my puja needs." Do you recall this incidence, Bipradasbabu?'

Bipradas said that he did.

Ashok resumed, 'She talked about many episodes till late in the evening, and then she finally said, "Masi was critical about their superstitions, and so was I once. But I am now confused about what is right and what is wrong. I had never thought twice about taking food from other people's hands—my lifelong belief was that it was awful, but now I am not so sure. My rational mind shames me for this, and I want no one to know about it, but when I remember that he does not approve of such misgivings, my heart turns against all that.'"

Bipradas felt uneasy as he listened to Ashok. With a forced smile, he remarked, 'Has Bandana begun to practise food taboos? Only the other day, she bragged that back at her masi's place, she had gone back to the customs and beliefs of her society and was relieved to be away from the many restrictive practices of the Mukhujye family.'

Ashok was about to respond, but before he could do so, Bandana came in and said, 'Mukhujyemashai, everything is arranged. We leave tomorrow by the 9:30 a.m. train, so please complete your puja and everything else before then. Sadly, God had destined all this trouble for you.'

'That may be the case,' Bipradas concurred with a smile.

'Not may be, but certainly. I wish someone was there to rescue you from such little problems! Anyway, I have arranged your breakfast for tomorrow. I will bring you your food and clothes, and then take you back to your home. You are still not fully fit. Ashokbabu, let us go now. I cannot touch your feet, Mukhujyemashai. It is regarded as superstition.' She smiled and left, raising her joint hands to her head.

TWENTY-TWO

They set off for Balarampur the next day. As they neared home, they observed that Dwijadas had made plans for his mother's pond dedication ceremony on a princely scale. Rows of temporary huts had been erected—some were still to be completed—on the field facing the house, and many of them were already occupied by the invitees. There was no counting as to how many visitors were still to arrive.

Ma was shocked when she saw Bipradas. 'What has gone wrong, son? You have lost so much weight!'

Bipradas touched his mother's feet and said, 'No need for any alarm. Now that I am here, I will be back to normal soon.'

When Bandana touched her feet, she blessed her and said, 'Welcome, child.'

Her voice lacked any warmth and was no more than the formal observation of common courtesy. She only knew that Bandana had not been invited and had come on her own. She then started talking about Maitreyee. To Dayamoyee, Maitreyee's accomplishments were endless, and her only regret was that she found it almost impossible to make a list of all her virtues.

She said, 'There is nothing that her father has not taught her; there is no work that she cannot handle. Bouma had not been keeping too well, and she took up all responsibilities. It was most fortunate that she came. I shudder to think what would have happened if she were not here.'

Bipradas said, 'Really, Ma?'

Dayamoyee nodded, 'True, absolutely true. From the way the girl performs her duties, it relieves me of my worries. With someone like her as a companion, Bouma will be able to carry out her obligations without any hitch. I missed it this year, but if I am alive, I am determined to visit Kailash next year with a relaxed mind.'

Bipradas said nothing. Perhaps, Dayamoyee's hymn of praises to Maitreyee was justified, but there should have been a limit as well as an appropriate time and place for it. Regardless of her motive, her pretext was quite obvious. An unkind, impatient meanness rudely shook her sense of dignity. Looking at her son, she appeared to have realized her error, but, by then, it was too late to make any amends. The situation was saved by the arrival of Dwijadas, who, hearing about Bipradas's arrival, left his work and promptly came to meet him.

Bipradas asked him, 'What a huge task have you taken on? Can you manage this?'

Dwijadas said, 'Dada, you declined this job and passed it on to me. So, what is your worry?'

Bandana chipped in, 'If this huge expenditure cannot be raised from the tenants, his funds will have to help out. That is the worry, Dijubabu.'

Everyone started laughing. The jest helped lighten Ma's heart, and she said with a touch of feigned indignation, 'Must you, like your didi, rag him? This son of mine is a very high-principled child of mine, and I cannot stand it when all of you go after him.'

Bandana answered, 'But Ma, if pinpricks are baseless, it should not then hurt anyone.'

Ma said, 'He does not get upset, he just smiles.'

Bandana riposted, 'Not without reason. Mukhujyemashai knows well that one can accept punishment as long as one's stomach is full. Right?'

Bipradas acceded, 'Of course, it is so. Equally, it is pointless to be riled by what fools say. Antidotes for this are prescribed in our ancient texts.'

'Hmm. Mejdi happens to be less literate than I am. And because of the prescriptions of your ancient texts, everyone regards you so highly,' Bandana smiled as she said this and turned her face away. Dwijadas was trying to suppress his amusement, and Dayamoyee also began to smile. She said, 'Bandana is a very naughty girl. No one can outsmart her.'

Later, she turned solemn and said, 'Listen to me, child, I can't say that during my husband's time, tenants were never coerced. But, as I told you, my Bipin is a very righteous man and he will not take what is not his due. I am not so sure about Diju.'

Bipradas protested, 'This is wrong of you, Ma. Does Diju exploit the tenants? Have you forgotten that he once took the side of the tenants and provoked them not to pay rents?'

Ma said, 'No. I have not, and that is why I say this. One who can incite tenants to not pay their rightful dues can also not scruple to exploit them. He is kind, perhaps excessively so, but you will find one day that the tenants will suffer much under his dispensation.'

'No, Ma, never.'

Dayamoyee said, 'The only saving grace is that you are here. He needs someone who can guide him along the right path. Or else, someday he will sink and take others down with him.'

Dwijadas had remained silent all this time, but reacted sharply to his mother's observation, 'Ma, your last words are not right. Yes, I may go down someday, but I can assure you I will not take others down with me.'

Dayamoyee replied, 'That is not really the issue. The real issue is that you need someone who can guide you.'

Dwijadas said, 'Why do you not clearly say that everyone would be relieved if I had someone to take me in hand? And, it seems that you have more or less fixed the problem.'

The significance of the conversation then became very clear to all.

Dayamoyee continued to speak, 'You never listened to anyone when you arranged this huge affair. All you said was that it was Dada's command. But did Dada ask you to undertake something like the Ashwamedh of the olden times? Who is going to take care of all this? Fortunately, Maitreyee is here. She is the most capable.'

Dwijadas said, 'Let this job be done, then you can hand out your certificates to whoever you wish to. What is the rush to do so now?

Bandana asked, 'Who will sign the certificates, Dijubabu? Not the third party, is it?'

Dwijadas said, 'How can the third party dare? Particularly, when the all-powerful first and second parties are both here?' And both of them laughed.

Ma and Bipradas looked at each other with no clue about their private joke.

Annada came in looking agitated and said, 'Bandanadidi, I cannot find the box in which you packed Barababu's medicines. I hope it is not lost.'

Dayamoyee was alarmed. 'What is to be done now, Bandana? That was a very serious lapse.'

Bandana assured her, 'That was not an oversight. I deliberately left them behind.'

'Deliberately left them behind? What do you mean?'

'I thought that he had taken far too many medicines for too long. He needed them as Ma was not there. But he does not need any medicine now. He will get well quickly now.'

Dayamoyee was delighted by those words. Even so, she said, 'I don't think what you did was proper. It is a village. We don't have good doctors. What if there is a need...'

Annada intervened, 'There won't be any need, Ma. If it were, she would have brought the medicines. She would have never left them behind. She knows much better than the doctors.'

Dayamoyee looked at Bandana with admiration. Bandana said, 'Ma, it is Anudi's nature to exaggerate. Truly, I know nothing. Whatever little I have learned was while I was looking after Mukhujyemashai.'

Annada added, 'Only I know the kind of care she took. One day I faced a serious situation. There was no one in the house. Diju had gone back home for Basu's illness. Dattamashai was away in Dhaka when Bipin came home running a temperature. I somehow managed for a couple of days, but his temperature kept shooting up. I sent for the doctor. He came and prescribed medicines, but also put the fear of death in us. Being an illiterate woman, I was at a loss as to what to do. I could not let you know, as Bipin stopped me. Distraught, I ran to Bandanadidi at her masi's house. With tears in my eyes, I told her, "Didi, please do not stay angry with us, please come with me. Your Mukhujyemashai is very ill." Without a word, she got into the car. She did not even wait to inform her masi. She came home and immediately took charge of Bipin. For several days, she did not get even an hour's rest. She didn't just give him his medicines, but did everything from setting up his puja things in the morning to putting him to bed at night, tucked inside the mosquito net. So, if Bandanadidi says no more medicines, do not oppose her. Bipin will get well.'

Bipradas immediately agreed, 'I will get well, Ma. Don't dissuade her. No more medicines for me.'

Dayamoyee gazed at them with love and affection reflecting in her eyes.

A maidservant walked in and said, 'Boudie wants to know where she should put the things that have arrived from Calcutta.'

Before Dayamoyee could give an answer, Bandana said, 'Just because I am your untouchable child, must I be denied any role in this big ceremony of yours and sit idle? Surely there is much to do, some of which may not get polluted by my touch?'

Dayamoyee drew Bandana close to her and taking off a bunch of keys from the end of her sari, she gave it to her and said, 'Why should I allow you to sit idle, child? Here, take this key to my personal storeroom, which I never give to anyone except Bouma. This is in your charge now.'

'What is kept in this storeroom?'

Dwijadas, identifying the familiar key, answered, 'The issue of caste pollution does not apply to the articles stored there—they are gold and silver, money, sacramental apparels, etc. Nothing that cannot be offered to the most spiritual of men, even if touched by you.'

Bandana asked, 'What will be my job, Ma?'

Dayamoyee said, 'To pay the scholar priests their honorarium, to ensure the appropriate reception of guests, to pay for the travel expenses of friends and relations, and, on top of that, to keep an eye on this lad of mine.' Pointing to Dwijadas, she said, 'Taking advantage of my ignorance of accounts, he has cheated me of endless sums of money that he squandered. You have to stop that.'

Dwijadas said, 'Ma, you ought not to talk like this in Dada's presence. He may assume that to be true. All expenses are faithfully recorded. You are welcome to check if you do not believe me.'

Dayamoyee said, 'It is true that expenses are being properly recorded, but who is keeping a record of the waste of money? That is precisely what I was trying to tell Bandana.'

Bandana was perplexed. 'But what do I gain by this knowledge? If he chooses to squander his own money, how do I stop him?'

Dayamoyee answered, 'That I do not know. You asked for a role, and I am happy to give you one. Let me tell you, Bandana. Some day, you will have to manage your own family. You cannot then get away by claiming ignorance of how to cope with the waste of money.'

Bandana told Dwijadas, 'Well, you have heard your mother's command!'

Dwijadas answered, 'Indeed, I have. Dada has put me in charge of the expenditure, while Ma has asked you to check the expenditure. So, clashes are inevitable. Don't blame me then.'

Bandana said with a smile, 'No question of that, Dijubabu. We won't get into a fight. I am not so immature as to get into a mock fight with you about your money. I have learnt so much after coming to Bengal. Before we get into a scrap, I will return Ma's charge to her and leave.'

Though Dayamoyee did not fully comprehend their dispute, she did believe that her grievance was justified. She said in a pained voice, 'No, child, I will not take back your responsibility. You will have to discharge it. Let us not delay any longer. Come with me, so that I can explain your duties to you.' She took Bandana away with her.

During her previous visit to the house, Bandana had been there for only a few hours. So, she had not had the opportunity to look closely at the place. She was awestruck now by the vast size of it with its endless numbers of apartments. There were many dependant relatives and many of them had their families there. On one side of the house were the office and connected facilities; on another side were the temple, the kitchen,

Dayamoyee's huge cowshed, and the high-walled garden and pond. They arrived at a room on the eastern wing of the first floor.

'This room is now your responsibility,' Dayamoyee told Bandana.

In a verandah of another wing, Sati and Maitreyee were engaged in carefully sorting out certain items. They looked up upon hearing Dayamoyee's voice and abandoned their work to greet Bandana. No one had really expected her there.

Bandana touched her didi's feet and greeted Maitreyee with a formal namaskar. Ma explained, 'This outcaste child of mine wanted to help with the work here, as she did not wish to sit idle. I have given you your various tasks, and I put her in charge of this store and gave her the key.'

'What do you keep in this store?' asked Maitreyee.

'Such things that will not get polluted even when touched by this outcaste girl,' Dayamoyee joked. She had Bandana unlock the room and they all went in. Stacks of silverware piled up on the floor were for the honorarium to brahmins and scholars, bags of coins for distribution to the poor, and bundles of sacramental clothes still to be unpacked. In addition to all that, there was a personal safe belonging to Dayamoyee, and, pointing it out to Bandana, she said, 'That safe contains all my personal valuables, and Diju has his eyes on this safe. You need to keep it under strict watch so that he cannot trick you as he does me.'

Looking at Bandana's worried face, Sati pleaded on her behalf, 'Ma, should you put such a major responsibility on

192

her? It involves so much money...' Before she could finish, Dayamoyee intervened, 'Precisely why I gave her the key, or else Diju will bankrupt me.'

'But, Ma, she is an outsider.'

Dayamoyee laughed and said, 'So were you when you arrived here, and so was I many years ago. That is not a problem. But I have no time now, I must go.' So saying, she left.

Bandana told Sati, 'I seem to have been inextricably trapped in your house, Mejdi. I don't think I will have a moment to breathe.'

Sati smiled and said, 'So it seems.'

TWENTY-THREE

Nobody can predict when and how disaster will strike a family. In the midst of all the work that was going on, Kalyani came to her mother, weeping, 'Ma, my husband tells me to go back with him to our home right away. Though no immediate train is available, he would prefer to wait at the railway station, but refuses to stay another minute in this house.'

The dedication ceremony of the pond was just over, and Ma had stepped out from the pavilion. Her daughter's voice confounded her. She could not follow what her daughter was saying. 'Who asked you to leave? Sasadhar? Why?'

'Baradada severely humiliated him and threw him out of his room,' Kalyani wept.

The house was humming with activity—people were being fed, music was being played, beggars were clamouring, and scholar-priests were splitting hairs over the scripture. In the midst of all the happenings burst forth the unsettling situation.

Sati and Maitrayee arrived. Bandana also followed after locking the storeroom. Many relatives and friends stood around as curious onlookers. Sasadhar came and told her, 'Ma, we are leaving. We came because you asked us, but sadly we cannot stay.'

'Why not, son?'

'Bipradasbabu turned me out of his room.'

'Why did he do that?'

'May be because he is a wealthy person. His conceit drives him blind. He presumed that it was easy to humiliate me in his own house. But do let him know that my father had left me a zamindari which is not meagre, and I do not have to go begging for my food.'

Dayamoyee was devastated. She said, 'Let me send for Bipin and I will ask him what the problem was. My function is not yet over; some jobs still remain to be done, but if you leave before then, I will drown myself in the very pond that I have just established.' Her eyes brimmed with tears.

But those tears had no effect on her son-in-law. Though he came from a decent family, neither his looks nor his nature were gentle. In fact, one shrank away from his company. With his large figure and face, he puffed up like an angry cat and declared, 'I can stay back only on one condition. Bipradasbabu will have to ask for my apology with folded hands in the presence of all here. Not otherwise.'

Everyone was stunned by that incredible suggestion. Bipradas to ask for apologies with folded hands! And that too publicly! All remained speechless until Sati said pleadingly, 'Not now please. Let the function end, Ma will settle this in the evening. How can anyone insult you? If he has done anything wrong, he will surely ask for your apologies.'

Bandana's eyes flared, but she spoke calmly, 'Mejdi, he is never wrong.'

Sati admonished her, 'Be quiet, Bandana. Anyone can be wrong.'

Bandana was firm, 'No, he can never be.'

That provoked Maitreyee who said sharply, 'How do you know? Were you present there? Is Sasadharbabu making up a story?'

'I never implied that. All I said was that Mukhjyemashai cannot do anything improper.'

In reply, Maitreyee said in a mocking tone, 'All men trangress. They are not God. He has even insulted my father.'

Bandana said, 'In that case, he should have also left like Sasadharbabu and not stayed back.'

Maitreyee retorted cuttingly, 'You are not owed any explanations. It has to be settled with Dijubabu who invited him here.'

Sati reprimanded Bandana, 'I beg of you, Bandana, go back to your work.'

Sasadhar told Dayamoyee, 'I am not here to talk about rights and wrongs. All I want to know is whether your son will apologize to me with folded hands or not. Otherwise, I will leave. I will not stay here for another minute. Your daughter may come with me or not—if not, she should forget her husband's home forever. Let us settle this here and now.'

How calamitous! Nothing was impossible for Sasadhar to do. In inviting her daughter and son-in-law, Dayamoyee had invited trouble. Kalyani continued to grieve. Dayamoyee did not know whom to approach for help. She was at her wits' end. She told her son-in-law, 'Somewhere something must have gone wrong, please wait. I will get Bipradas here. With the house full of guests and visitors, if this calumny becomes public, I will have no option but to take my own life.'

Sasadhar said, 'Fair enough, let him come. Let him lie if he wishes to deny what he has done.'

'Bipradas never lies,' she said, as she sent for him. Bipradas arrived soon, appearing as usual—peaceful, solemn, and self-controlled. Only his eyes had a touch of weariness—it was difficult to fathom what was behind them.

Dayamoyee asked, 'What is this I hear from Sasadhar? That you turned him out of your room? Is that true?'

Bipradas said, 'Yes, it is true, Ma.'

'You turned my son-in-law out of your room despite the fact that I have this ceremony?'

'Yes, Ma, it is true that I asked him to leave my room. I also told him never again to enter my room.'

Dayamoyee looked stunned. 'But why?'

'It is better for you to not know, Ma.'

Sati could not keep quiet. She appealed anxiously to her husband, 'We are not interested in knowing why, but Sasadharbabu proposes to leave this house immediately with Kalyani. Just think of the scandal that will follow. Tell him that you have made a mistake. Please ask him not to leave.'

Bipradas glanced at his wife for an instant and then said, 'Sati, I do not make impetuous mistakes.'

'Yes, you do, everyone does. Please ask them to stay.'

'I have made no mistake.'

Dayamoyee had been quiet while Bipradas and his wife were talking, but at that moment, she spoke up, sharp and forceful, 'Leave this argument about what is right and what is wrong. I cannot accept that my daughter and son-in-law will go away from me forever. Go and ask for Sasadhar's apologies.'

'No, Ma, it is not possible.'

'I am not concerned about the possible and the impossible. You have to ask for Sasadhar's apologies.'

Bipradas remained quiet. It dawned on Dayamoyee that there was no way that she could turn the impossibility into a possibility. She flared up and said, 'This house does not belong only to you, and my husband never gave you the authority to turn out anyone. They will stay here.'

Bipradas said, 'Ma, if you had told me of your decision instead of sending for me, then I would have kept quiet, but now I cannot. If Sasadhar stays here, I will have to leave. Never to return. It is for you to decide, Ma.'

Never had she faced such a dilemma in her life. Her daughter and son-in-law were on one side, and Bipin on the other. Bipin was the child she had brought up, who was dearest to her, her last resort at times of distress, the child whom she held the closest. But he would not waver from his resolution. There was no recourse, no turning back, and the after-effects were inevitable, as destined. Even so, she could not control herself and her rage egged her on. She said bitterly, 'You are unfairly obstinate. I cannot abandon my daughter and son-in-law for life because of your obstinacy. This is not possible. Do whatever you wish. Come, Sasadhar, come with me. No need to pay any heed to him. This is not only his house.' She collected Sasadhar and Kalyani and took them away. Maitreyee followed them, as if she were one of them.

It was feared that the episode would unnerve Sati; but, to the surprise of both Bandana and Bipradas, she appeared solidly steady. She had turned pale and said, 'I have no idea what Sasadharbabu has done, and I also know that you would not have allowed this serious occurrence without any reason. Believe me, I will never hold you responsible for what has happened.'

Bipradas did not speak. Sati asked him, 'Will you be leaving today?'

'No, tomorrow.'

'And never come back?'

'So it seems.'

'What about me and Basu?'

'You will also have to leave. If not tomorrow, then some other day.'

'Not some other day, we will also go with you tomorrow.' Turning to Bandana, she asked, 'What will you do, Bandana? Leave tomorrow?'

Bandana said, 'I am not a party to this dispute, so I do not have to follow you.'

Sati said, 'Neither I nor my husband had any part in this. But where he has no place, I also have none. Not even for a day. You would have appreciated this had you been married.'

'I do not have to be married to appreciate this. But mistakes can be made, and I cannot understand your decision to support your husband without getting to the bottom of this affair.'

'You would have if you had a husband,' saying so, Sati left, trying to stem her tears.

Bandana turned to Bipradas and asked, 'What have you done, Mukhujyemashai?'

'I had no option, Bandana.'

'But this separation from your mother? I can hardly imagine it.'

Bipradas said, 'True, but when new issues raise their heads, one has to look for fresh solutions. But one still moves ahead. Do not try to stop your mejdi. She will go with me. But what about you? Are you planning to stay here for a few more days?'

Bandana replied, 'I really do not know. In the face of new situations, I will seek my answer following the old system, the system that I first confronted when I arrived suddenly in this house, the like of which I had never seen, the system that wrought a permanent change in my ideas.'

Bipradas did not react except with a little smile on his lips—a smile that reflected both pain and despair. 'I must leave now, but we will meet again.'

Tears flooded Bandana's eyes. She said, 'If I see you again, I will greet you from a distance. Harsh is your nature, and hard your heart with no room for love and clemency. In case I do not have another opportunity, let me tell you this. May I learn to treat as my own those whose lives get intimately entwined with mine. Let me not run after a will-o'-the-wisp. When I think of you from afar, I will tell myself—he is untarnished; he is faultless; he is great. No one can leave a scratch on his stony heart. He is unique in this world. He can call no one as his own, nor can anyone call him their own.'

It was very late in the night when all work relating to the function was over. It had been a very hectic day. Everything ran as clockwork within the well-disciplined system of that household. But nobody knew that the core of the system then lay in tatters. After her duties in the storeroom, Bandana was returning to her room when she noticed that the lights were still on in Dwijadas's room. She hesitated, since it would be improper to go into his room at that hour, but the thought that she had been nursing through the day propelled her to go in. At the door, she asked, 'Dijubabu, have you gone to bed yet?'

Dwijadas replied from the room, 'No, not yet, but what brings you here now?'

'May I come in?'

'Please do.'

Bandana pushed open the door and entered the room. She found Dwijadas sitting up on the bed surrounded by heaps of papers. She asked, 'Going through today's accounts? Accounts can wait, but staying up too late might affect your health.'

'That then would be a relief. I won't have to bother about these,' said Dwijadas.

'Have the expenses been too high? Do you have to explain a lot to Dada?'

He pushed aside the papers, sat up on the bed, and said, 'The wheel of life goes round—happy days following days of distress. By God's grace, times have changed. I do not have to be answerable to my dada. On the contrary, I can ask him for explanations. I will ask him to render me the accounts, bring me money, and tell me what he has been doing.'

Bandana was puzzled. 'What is the matter?'

Dwijadas raised both his arms with folded hands and said, 'It is very serious and deep. By the grace of my mother, aided and abetted by my brother-in-law Sasadhar, I can now warn Bipradas and tell him—"Be careful, Bipradas. I will destroy you. You cannot escape from my hand."'

Though frightfully disturbed, Bandana laughed and said, 'Must you joke always? Can you not be serious even for a moment?'

Dwijadas said, 'Can't I? Get Sasadhar here—no, let him be. You will find that my jokes will vanish in a trice. My face will turn wild and fearsome. Just test me.'

Bandana pulled up a chair and asked, 'So you know it all?'

'Not all, just a little. Dada knows everything, but he is like a deep forest. Sasadhar is the other one who knows everything, but he will lie.'

Bandana asked anxiously, 'Can you not tell me whatever you know? I am really alarmed.'

Dwijadas said, 'It is pointless to get scared. Dada's resolution is unshakeable. He is lost to us.' Tears welled up in his eyes.

Bandana asked, 'Can a separation happen so easily? Can you not prevent it?'

Dwijadas shook his head, 'No. When a rift comes, it comes so swiftly that it brooks no barrier. The unhappy ones who shed tears will continue to do so, and that is the end of the story. I don't know the details. I will tell you whatever I know; and if I need help, I will come to your door wherever you are.'

'Why to me only?'

'When I need help, I can only go to the good and the great, as our holy books say.'

'But is there no one else great?'

'There may be, but I do not know them. I won't talk about Dada, but whenever I needed help, I had always gone to Boudie. Sadly, that road is now closed to me. You are her sister, and my claim on you is based on that connection.'

'What about Ma?'

'Ma is unparalleled as a charioteer when the chariot runs smoothly, but she is helpless when the chariot gets stuck in a rut. In such distressed days, I will approach you for help. Will you refuse me?'

'How can I answer if I do not know the nature of the help you need?'

'Neither do I, but I shall not seek your help unless direly needed. I will come to you when there is no other recourse.'

'Will you not tell me what I want to know?'

Dwijadas said, 'I do not know the whole story, and whatever I know may not be absolutely true. But I do know something which is beyond any doubt—Dada is now destitute; he has lost everything.'

Bandana was shocked. 'Mukhujyemashai is destitute? How did this happen?'

Dwijadas told her, 'Very easily, because of Sasadhar's scheming. The day Saha-Choudhuri Company went bankrupt, all of Dada's fortunes went down that hole. This story is for public consumption. What remains hidden is another history.'

Bandana cried out in alarm, 'Forget history! Give me the

facts. Is it true that Dada is destitute?'

'That is true. There is no mistake there.'

'What about Mejdi and Basu? Are they also impoverished?'

'Yes, except for Boudie's allowance from her father. A very small amount.'

'But Mukhjyemashai will never touch it.'

'No, he would rather fast, which he is used to.'

Bandana asked, 'What about you? Are you not affected?'

'Fear not,' Dwijadas replied, 'I am well-secured. Dada sunk himself, but kept me afloat. If you ask me how this was possible, it is because of my mother's intelligence, Dada's honesty, and perhaps my lucky stars. Let me recount the facts. Sasadhar was in school with Dada. They were very close to each other. After they grew up, Dada negotiated his marriage with our sister Kalyani. This was a great achievement of Dada. It was reported that Sasadhar's father was a substantial zamindar—very affluent— and, on top of that, they had a sizeable flourishing business enterprise. There was no rival matching their vast fortune in Pabna. Four years later, Sasadhar told us that all his wealth, including his estate as well as their business enterprise, was going down the drain and he needed protection. Ma agreed, but she also told him, "Diju is still a minor, so his property cannot be touched." When Sasadhar claimed that he would be able to settle his loan in a year, Ma wished him luck but still insisted that her husband had left strict instructions not to use the minor's money.

'Kalyani came crying to Dada, "You got us married, but can you bear to see me begging on the streets with my children?

I know Ma can, but can you?"

'Kalyani hit at his most vulnerable spot—his faith, his doctrine, his conscience, his altruism. He comforted her and told her to go home with the assurance that he would do her best to help her. Kalyani returned home and the history thereafter is now known. But look, it is almost dawn now.' He gazed out of the window.

Bandana got up to leave. Looking at the heaps of paper, she asked, 'What are those?'

'Oh, they are the documents that protect my future. Dada brought them with him when he came here. May I ask if you too are planning to leave today?'

'I do not know for sure, but we will meet again.' She left thereafter.

TWENTY-FOUR

Forcing Sati to sit down on a chair, Bandana applied red dye (alta) on her feet. After instructing Bandana about how to perform the ritual, Annada had gone into hiding. 'I cannot show my face to Sati,' she said.

'Why not, Anudi?' Bandana asked.

'Why could I not have died before this happened? I did not just raise Diju. I also raised Bipin. When his mother died, in whose hands did she leave the two-month-old child? Mine. Where was Dayamoyee then? And her daughter and son-in-law?' She left, covering her weeping eyes.

As Bandana applied alta to her sister's feet, Sati felt a drop of warm tear on her foot. She bent down, wiped Bandana's eyes with her hand, and asked, 'Why are you crying, Bandana?'

'So is everyone, Mejdi, not just me,' said Bandana in a choked voice.

'Just because everyone is crying, must you also? With your education, what kind of an explanation is this?'

Bandana looked up and said, 'So one must weep only after offering a reason, is it? What sort of logic is this, Mejdi?'

Sati affectionately fondled Bandana's head and said, 'No point in arguing with a logician, but that was not my point. They are all shedding tears because they believe I have now lost everything, but that is not true. I have my husband, I have my son. So I have suffered no loss. Do not grieve for me. I am not despondent.'

Bandana said, 'May no adversity ever touch you, but that is not all that matters. You probably know the extent of your loss, but what about those who continue to shed tears in anguish for you? Who is going to console them?'

She mused for a bit and continued, 'Mukhujyemashai is a man, let him follow his own dictates. But I pray, Didi, when you go, do not go with your eyes dry. It will distress them awfully.'

'Who will be distressed, Bandana?'

'Are you asking me who they are? Do you not know them? When you came into this family at the age of nine, those who embraced you and for years made you their own, have you forgotten them just because of this one shock? Your mother-in-law, your brother-in-law, the servants, the resident relations, the temple, your guest house—do you think your husband and son will compensate for their absence? Is there nothing else in life?'

Bandana went on, 'Do you know whose words these are? Of the environment in which you and I grew up. Do you believe that devotion to one's husband is the last word? That there is nothing beyond that? You are wrong. Come with me to my masi's house in Calcutta. Such beliefs there are considered old—they do not accept them. And yet...,' she stopped talking.

207

They felt that someone was behind them. Turning back, they saw it was Dwijadas. They had no inkling when he had walked in quietly. Bandana tried to say something in embarassment, but Dwijadas intervened and said, 'Fear not. I do not know your masi or anyone in her group, so they will not know what you are saying about them. Animals have their groups, and their life runs according to a formula. But humans do not; the law of groups does not apply to them. This thought has been occupying my mind all morning. Pulling away from your masi's group, you can easily get into my dada's company and equally take Maitreyee out of my mother's grip. She can be easily absorbed into your masi's party. I can wager that this can happen with ease. Strange is men's heart, stranger their nature.'

Sati was bewildered, 'What are you saying, Thakurpo?'

'You are asking me to explain what I mean? If what Diju does and says made any sense, why would he then have run to you for so long with his appeals instead of running to Dayamoyee or Bipradas? It is because you don't have the urge to understand, right? Now that you are leaving, let us leave it that way.' He then bent down and placed his head on Sati's feet. He rarely did that. The dye of the still-wet alta stained his forehead, and he stopped Sati from wiping it, saying, 'The stain will go, Boudie, on its own, but let it stay for the time being.' Diju spoke light-heartedly, but Bandana's eyes filled with tears and she turned away as he spoke.

Dwijadas said, 'I came here to rush you. It is time for you to leave. Dada is fretting. Your baggage had already been sent on. Basu has been dressed and waiting in the car. I do not know who organized this ritual, but I'm glad that it was done. I was afraid that Anudi may have died. But no, she must be somewhere, or else, who could have fixed all this? Mother has locked herself in her room, but nothing can be done to help her get over this crisis. You can speak to Maitreyee if you wish to, who will then convey your words to Ma. But I say, there is no need for that. Better look sharp and get into the car. After seeing you off at the railway station, I can return to my work.'

Sati smiled sadly and said, 'Thakurpo can't wait to see me leave.'

'I have my work to do.'

'What work?'

'Better not ask, for it is not suitable for your ears. Anyway, you never asked me questions earlier. You simply gave me whatever I asked for.'

Sati and Bandana both looked at him for a while and then Sati said, 'Thakurpo, go ahead. I won't be late.' Turning to Bandana, she said, 'Do not stay here, little sister. Go back to Bombay as early as you can. There is no need to return to Calcutta. Don't forget, Uncle is all by himself in Bombay.'

Like Diju, Bandana placed her head on Sati's feet and told her, 'No, I am not going back to Masi. I am done with them. I may return to Bombay tomorrow, but before you go, do assure me that we shall meet soon again.'

Sati blessed her and replied, 'But that is in your hands. Tell Uncle to invite us to your marriage. We will go there from wherever we are.' She deliberated for a while about whether she should say what she had in mind, and then said, 'It was my dearest wish that you would also come to this family and get married to Thakurpo. I would then hand over the responsibility of this home to you, put Basu in your charge, and go on a pilgrimage with Ma to Kailash. If I cannot return from there, then I won't. But we humans desire one thing, and what happens is something else.' She paused and then went on, 'What I have received here is very rare. Very few can be so fortunate. My most precious gift has been my mother-in-law, and yet the breakup with her has been the most bitter. I could not meet her before I go. She has locked herself in. So I paid homage by placing my head on the floor before her door.' She broke down as she spoke. She said a little later, 'I also missed seeing my Anudi. She has been more than a mother to me. Tell her that I am very upset. And my pet cat, Nimu. I don't know where she is. Talk to Anudi about her, Bandana.' Yet earlier, she had declared strongly that she had her husband and son with her, so she had lost nothing. How false that had proved to be!

'Boudie, what on earth are you doing?' Dwijadas came to hurry her along.

'Yes, yes, I'm on my way,' said Sati and quickly left.

By the time Dwijadas returned from the railway station, it was well into evening. Lamps had been lit in the rooms and the domestic staff were all engaged in discharging their respective duties, but no one had any idea of the upheaval that had rocked the house. The doors and windows of Bipradas's sitting room were closed, but that was not unusual as Bipradas was often away in Calcutta. Ashok occupied the room to the left of the staircase, where he was seen reading. Akshaybabu was still there, giving his college a miss, but no one knew whether he was in his room or had gone for a walk. Stepping out of the car, Dwijadas observed that there was a light in the library, which would normally have been dark at that time. He had no doubt that Bandana was there, not to read but to dry her eyes. She had isolated herself to avoid meeting people. The next day, she would travel far away to Bombay where her father lived and where she had grown up. There, she had her many relatives and friends. That she would be ever back to the village on some pretext was inconceivable. Probably not, yet she would not easily forget that place. Diju recollected everything from the day she had arrived unexpectedly and left abruptly. All they had done was to talk for an hour or so. Bandana had told him then rather amusedly, 'We may not have met until now, but Mejdi told us all about her brother-in-law in her letters. Nothing about you is unknown to me. The way you used to irritate your family has all been reported to me. I know everything.' To which Diju had reacted, 'Since we did not know each other, what was the point of maligning me to you?' Bandana had laughed and said, 'Perhaps Mejdi cannot stand you, and this was a kind of revenge.'

They had both laughed together at those words, not knowing that her letters had been Sati's ploy to attract Bandana towards Diju; if only she could have her sister close to her and succeed in getting Bandana and her wayward brother-in-law together. But that was not to be. Her heart's desire remained locked in her heart, and those two never understood the real significance of her letters.

Dwijadas went up and, on entering the library, he found Bandana with an open book in her hand, looking out of the window. He doubted if she had at all looked at the book, but just to start a conversation, he asked, 'What are you reading?'

Bandana closed the book and asked, 'It took you a while to get back. The Calcutta-bound train should have left long ago.'

Dwijadas said, 'It may be late, but I am back. I might not have returned at all.'

'True enough.'

'The thought did strike me. When the train left, little Basu started waving his hand and disappeared round a bend. I felt that perhaps I should have gone with them.'

Bandana asked, 'You are very attached to Basu, are you not?'

Dwijadas pondered for a while and said, 'I really do not know what to say. I suspect that true feelings are probably beyond me, against my nature. My heart is so harsh and arid that these sentiments do not last long enough. While at the railway station, my eyes did fill with tears, but only momentarily.'

'That is actually a blessing,' said Bandana.

Dwijadas said, 'It could be. I really do not know. It is on account of Basu that Ma locked herself in. It has nothing to do with Dada or Boudie. Ma believes that it was she who has brought Basu up, but if you think about it, you will find that for half his life, Ma has been away on pilgrimage. With whom did he stay then? With me. When he was down with typhoid for sixty days, who looked after him? I did. Who dressed him when he left this morning? I did. His clothes were kept in my cupboard and my table was the place for his books and papers. He sleeps in my bed. Ma would often drag him away, but on so many nights, he would wake up and come back to my bed.'

Bandana said, 'And still your eyes dried up in an instant.'

'Yes, it is my nature. My main concern is Basu, who will now be entirely in the hands of his parents. But that is only natural, you will say, so what is my worry? That is precisely my cause of worry. This is so natural. How can I convince people that the opposite is true?'

Bandana did not ask him the reason of doing so. On the other hand, his grievance against Basu's parents was unconvincing, particularly where Bipradas was concerned. But she did not argue the point.

Perhaps, to make his point clear, Dwijadas observed, 'One saving grace is that Boudie will be there. I would have no peace of mind leaving him to Dada only.'

'Being a detached person, why are you so worried about Basu? What will happen will happen.'

Dwijadas was hurt, but kept quiet.

Bandana teased him, 'Did you not tell me of your great respect and your deep faith in your dada? Did that vanish instantly like the tears in your eyes? Are you telling me that one who gets bankrupted through his own folly cannot be trusted?'

Dwijadas shot a painful look at her, but spoke softly, 'No, I did not insinuate that. All that I intended to say is that let not a thirsty person go begging to the sea. But no more talk about Dada. Outsiders will not comprehend it.'

This time, Bandana was hurt, but not knowing what to say, she kept quiet.

Dwijadas digressed from the topic, 'Are you returning to Bombay tomorrow?'

Bandana nodded.

'Is Ashokbabu taking you?'

'Yes.'

Dwijadas said, 'The mail train to Bombay leaves fairly late at night. I will go and see you off. Sorry, I will not be here in the morning as I have other commitments.'

'Can you please send a telegram to Father?'

'I will.'

Dwijadas was in two minds about what he wanted to say. 'I often think of asking something, but never can get round to it. You will be off tomorrow, so I may not get a chance. May I ask if it does not offend you?'

'Go ahead, tell me.'

He continued to waver.

'I will not be offended. Please tell me.'

Dwijadas asked, 'Can you recall that day when Ma was very upset and abruptly left Calcutta along with Boudie?'

'Yes, I do.'

'You were surprised and felt very bad, as you did not know the reason for her departure. You came to me and told me that you liked me. Can you remember that?'

'I do, embarrassingly so.'

'Did that mean anything?'

'No.'

'I thought as much.'

Pausing a little, he asked, 'I understand from Boudie that your masi wishes you to marry Ashok. Is that finally decided?'

Bandana said, 'This concerns our family. I can't discuss it with outsiders.'

'I did not wish to discuss it. I merely wanted information.'

Bandana said bitingly, 'We are not so closely related that you can raise such issues, Dijubabu. You are an educated person, so this curiosity on your part is shameful.' Dwijadas really did feel ashamed. 'Yes, I was wrong. By nature, I am not inquisitive; neither am I particularly interested in others. Somehow, though, I felt that I could tell you what I could not tell anyone else. When in trouble, I cannot go begging for help from anyone, but I can come to you. Yet, you...'

Bandana cut in with a smile, 'But you were the one who just said that you were unwilling to talk about your Dada with others? Meaning that I was a rank outsider.'

Dwijadas said, 'Because you hurt me, accusing me of my lack of respect for him. Do you not know what is going on inside me?' Tears were clearly visible in his eyes.

Maitreyee rushed in and said, 'Dwijababu, none of us know that you had returned.'

Dwijadas turned around and said, 'Why was that information so urgently needed?'

Maitreyee said, 'What are you saying? You ate nothing yesterday, nor today. Others may not know this, but I do. Come, let us go to Ma's room.'

'Isn't her door shut?'

Maitreyee said, 'It was, but it is not now. I got her to open the door with great effort. I had her have a bath and say her prayers, and then persuaded her to eat some fruits. She insisted that she would not eat until you did, but I told her that I was not going to listen to her. We have been waiting for you since then. Come to Ma's room, your food awaits you there.'

Dwijadas was astonished. He had never known Maitreyee to have talked so much. 'Let's go,' he said.

Turning to Bandana, she said, 'Please come with us. Ma has been asking about you.' She led Dwijadas away as though he had been arrested. Bandana followed them.

Dayamoyee was lying on her bed. It was painful to look upon her grief-stricken face. Kalyani was massaging her head. Sasadhar and Akshaybabu occupied two chairs. As Dwijadas entered the room, her body was wracked with sobs. Bandana sat by her feet. Never had she imagined such a painful moment. The silence was broken by Sasadhar. 'I believe you have been without food since yesterday. Do have something to eat.'

Dwijadas said, 'I will.'

Maitreyee cleared a place on the floor and was arranging Diju's food. Sasadhar asked, 'Why did you return so late? They left by the afternoon train?'

'Yes.'

Sasadhar said with a mock smile, 'Though I believe that the Calcutta house belongs to you.'

Dwijadas said, 'Is Dada not allowed to enter my house?'

Sasadhar said, 'I did not mean that, but he himself gave that impression. There was no need for him to leave this house. He could have made a compromise.'

Dwijadas said, 'If the road to compromise was open, then why did you not?'

Sasadhar spoke with a great deal of surprise, 'Why did I not compromise? What are you saying? Your brother insulted me and I should come to an understanding with him? A strange proposal!'

He started to laugh, and when he stopped, Dwijadas said, 'It is not a bad suggestion. Women have a saying—to live in the protection of a mountain. My dada was that protective mountain, and you lived in his protection. He has gone, and we are facing each other—you and I. The game is not over yet—it has just begun.'

'What do mean?'

'Just this—I am not Bipradas, your childhood friend. I am Dwijadas.'

Sasadhar's mocking smile disappeared. He said gravely, 'Can you explain what you mean by that?'

'Yes, I will. I should come clean,' Dwijadas replied. 'My dada is one of those who is willing to lose everything in the pursuit of truth, who would cut flesh from his own body to protect those who depend on them, who believes in something known as idealism. There is nothing that such men will not do for its sake. It is a kind of madness—and that is their misfortune. But I am a very normal man, no different from you. Like you, I can be violent; I have dislikes; I am thirsty for revenge. So if you have cheated my dada, I will also cheat you. If you have forged Dada's signature, I will send you to jail without hesitation— at least, I shall do my best until both of us are reduced to penury. This is how it always ends according to wise people. So, let it be thus.'

Sasadhar shouted, 'Ma, did you hear what Diju said? Please ask him not to say whatever comes to his mind!'

Dwijadas laughed, 'Complaining to Ma will be futile, Sasadharbabu. Ma knows that Diju does not regard what his mother says as the holy truth, as her Bipin did. Ma also knows well that Diju does not feign his defiance.'

217

They both ceased to speak and others remained quiet out of fear. It did not take Sasadhar long to realize that it was not a joke, but a case of firm resolve. When he tried to speak again, his voice had lost its earlier vigour, but he did manage to say somewhat strongly, 'This is the end. I shall not even have a drink of water here.'

Dwijadas said, 'What surprises me is how you could have even now!'

Kalyani started weeping. 'Will you, my own brother, ruin us?'

Dwijadas said, 'You believe that you can keep calamity away through your tears? And that time and again, there will be no sense of justice, and you will win? Dada is not here. Come to me when you have no food in your stomach. I will listen to you then, not now.'

Dayamoyee had endured all of that silently, but no longer. She screamed at Diju and said, 'Leave me! Who taught you to be so abusive? Bipin?'

'Did you say Bipin?'

'Yes, Bipin, who else?'

Dwijadas said, 'I shall leave you now. Ma, you have already stooped very low. Don't stoop any lower.'

A couple of hours after Dwijadas had returned to his room, Maitreyee entered with a tray of food. 'I had this food freshly cooked for you. Do sit down and eat,' she said.

'Who asked you to do all this?'

'No one, but do you think I am unaware of the fact that you have had nothing to eat since yesterday?'

'How is it that with so many people around, this was something you needed to know?

Maitreyee said nothing. Receiving no reply, Dwijadas said, 'Please put the food over there. I don't feel hungry now. I will eat when I am hungry.'

Maitreyee put the food down, carefully covering the dishes. She did not even tell him that he might not like the food if it turned cold.

Around midnight, Dwijadas stood up and, intending to eat a little something, went out of the room to wash his hands. He found someone sitting near the door, but could not recognize the person in the dim light. He asked, 'Who is there?'

'It is me, Maitreyee.'

Surprised, he asked, 'What are you doing here so late at night?'

'I was sitting here in case you needed something while you were eating.'

'That is not right at all. As it is, I need nothing; even if I do, is there no one else at home?'

Maitreyee replied softly, 'After the hard labour of the last few days, everyone is tired and has gone to bed.'

'But this applies to you as well, so why are you up?'

Maitreyee kept quiet. Dwijadas spoke in a comparatively tender voice, 'It does not look good for you to stand out there. Come into my room and supervise my meal.' He went out to wash his hands.

Dwijadas had rarely spoken to Maitreyee. The need had never arisen, nor did he sought to. When he returned, wondering how to talk to her, he found both his food and Maitreyee gone. She returned soon and said, 'I found that the food had gone cold, so I went to bring a fresh supply.'

Dwijadas said, 'Indeed, it is all warm, but how did you manage to do this so late at night?'

Maitreyee replied, 'I had arranged it earlier. When you told me that you might eat later, I thought then that the food I had kept in the room might turn cold.'

He praised the food and was told that much of it was her handiwork. She insisted him to have more helpings of the dishes he most enjoyed. She was clearly adept at the art of feeding people.

Dwijadas protested, 'Overeating may make me sick.'

'No, it will not. You've eaten nothing since yesterday, and you aren't eating that much now.'

'Surely, I am not the only one going without food in this house. There must be many more.'

Maitreyee said, 'I have no idea who these others are, but I do know how difficult it was to get Ma to eat anything at all.'

'Any news of Anudi?' asked Dwijadas.

Maitreyee was puzzled. 'What can be wrong with her? Is she also going without food?'

Until then, he had found talking to Maitreyee reasonably pleasant, but that annoyed him. 'You should not talk about Anudi in this manner. You may have been told she is only a maidservant. In this house, we do not consider anyone to be superior to her. She has brought us up after all.'

Maitreyee replied, 'Yes, I know that. But it is not uncommon in most houses for old retainers to bring up children. What is so new about that? Anyway, after you finish eating, I will look her up.'

Dwijadas looked at her for sometime, and it occurred to him that while it indeed was common in many families, outsiders who were not familiar with such relationships could understandably find them odd. His initial harsh reaction then softened and he said, 'Please do not worry about her. Anudi is unlikely to eat so late at night even if she has had nothing to eat earlier.'

After a while, he asked, 'From whom did you learn to look after people who are not your family members? From your mother?'

Maitreyee replied, 'No, from my didi. I have never known anyone who takes such good care of her husband.'

Dwijadas laughed, 'But a husband is a family member. I meant people who are not your own.'

'Not my own?' She lowered her eyes demurely.

'Well then, tell me about your didi.'

'My didi died three years ago, leaving behind a son and two daughters. Chaudhurimashai, her husband, did not even wait for a year to remarry. How disgraceful!'

Dwijadas said, 'Men are like that, unfazed about injustices.'

'Will you also do something like that?'

'Well, let me get married first. The question of remarriage arises later.'

Maitreyee protested, 'That is no way to talk. Your boudie has now left, so who will look after your mother?'

'I have no idea,' said Dwijadas. 'Perhaps, her daughter and son-in-law will, or perhaps someone else will arrive to take care of her. Nobody knows how impossibilities turn into possibilities in life. Let's not talk about us anymore. Tell me about yourself.'

'There is nothing to say.'

'Nothing? Nothing at all?'

Maitreyee shrank and said, 'Ah! Did someone tell you about Chaudhurimashai? What a shame! After my didi's death, he sent a proposal to my parents offering to marry me.'

'And then?'

Maitreyee said, 'Chaudhurimashai is very well off, so my parents agreed. They thought that at least Lila's children would be taken care of, as if I have no mission in life other than to take care of Didi's children. I told them that if they insisted, I would take my own life.'

'But why? Why such strong opposition?'

'Why not? Can there be anything more outrageous in life?'

Dwijadas said calmly, 'I am not one with you there, Maitreyee. It is not always so. For instance, my mother brought up my dada.'

Maitreyee said, 'But what is the outcome? Has anything more tragic ever happened to this family than today's incident?'

Dwijadas was silenced. She was not wrong, nor was she entirely right. He stirred and said, 'I will not deny it. A great tragedy has engulfed this family, I agree, but I know that what you have expressed is no more than women's normal reactions to trivial matters in a family.' Since he had finished eating by that time, he got to his feet.

Dwijadas was out on chores the next afternoon. It was dark when he returned. He went straight up to Bandana's room and asked, 'May I come in?'

'Is that you, Dijubabu? Please do come in.'

He found that Bandana had almost finished her packing, and all necessary travel arrangements had been made. 'So you are truly leaving. Could I not persuade you to stay for even one more day?'

It was not Bandana's wish initially to say anything, but she had to when she looked at him. 'Since I have to go anyway, what would be the point of staying another day?'

Dwijadas said, 'That was not the way I looked at it. The only thought that occupied my mind is that with everyone gone, I will have no friend left in this big house.'

Bandana said, 'Friends come and they go; that is the way of the world. One needs to be patient in that hope—there is no point in being restless.'

Dwijadas did not react.

Bandana said, 'I do not have much time, so let me tell you a few important things. You may have heard that Sasadharbabu has left?'

'No I had not, but I did guess as much.'

'Before they left, they refused to consume anything—they didn't even have a drop of water. They both touched Ma's feet and took their leave. After that, Ma turned her face away.' Bandana did not refer to last night's affair.

She reflected a bit and continued, 'Ma is in very bad shape. I really feel sorry for her—she is far too mortified to show her face to anyone. The way Maitreyee is looking after her is more than one's own daughter does. If Ma recovers, it will be wholly due to her. She is a very fine girl. Try to keep her a little longer.'

'Fine, I will try.'

'Can I leave you with one more request?'

'Yes, do.'

'You should get married.'

'Why?'

'Otherwise, this huge family will collapse. You have lost a great deal, but what remains is not insignificant. Just think about it—your wide network of charities, the noble deeds, the relatives who live under your protection, the support you offer to countless numbers of the poor and needy—these are not of recent origin. These traditions run long uninterrupted and deep in your family. But will all that end now? You have more than enough for your needs, despite what has been lost due to Dada's error. Accept what he has left you with as more than adequate. I trust that your inexhaustible and bountiful resources will not leave you in want of anything, and that will be my prayer for you before I go.'

Dwijadas's eyes filled with tears as he listened to her.

Bandana resumed, 'Your father left the management of all his property in the hands of your dada with supreme confidence. Because it did not work out, your dada is filled with guilt. If his failure wrecks the estate and destroys all the good work, Mukhujyemashai will never be able to live with himself. You have to save Dada from that misery.'

Controlling his tears, Dwijadas said, 'How strange! No one has ever felt for Dada in this way. Not even I.' It was fortunate that Bandana's face was in the shadows and he could not see her expression at that moment. He said, 'I can take all of Dada's sufferings on myself, but how can I undertake to carry on the burden of all the work he did? I do not feel brave enough. I went out today to check all the work that Dada was concerned with—schools for the various communities, not just one, but many! There are drainage canals that need to be built and are a long-term liability; and I have also come across a long list of his charities and donations—all outflows of resources. I do not know what to say when they ask for money.'

Bandana said, 'Assure them that they will receive their due. They have to be paid. Tell me, did he never share any of these with anyone?'

'No.'

'And why was that?'

Dwijadas said, 'It was not to keep his good deeds under wraps, but with whom could he have shared? He had no friends. He bore his unhappiness by himself, as also his happiness. He may have shared it with his one and only friend,' he pointed skywards, 'but how would we know about it? Only he and his inner God know.'

Bandana asked inquisitively, 'Tell me, Dijubabu, do you think Mukhujyemashai has ever loved anyone?'

Dwijadas replied, 'That would be against his nature. I don't think there is anyone in this world as lonely as he is.'

They were both silent. Then Bandana said, 'In any event, you will have to take over all his work. You cannot leave out even one of his tasks.'

'But I am not like my dada. How can I do all this by myself?'

'You cannot. You will have to get married.'

'How can I marry if I am not in love?'

Bandana looked at him in amazement and said, 'What are you saying, Dijubabu? One would say such things in our society, but whoever in your family married after falling in love? Put away such ideas!'

Dwijadas agreed, 'True, it is not a system followed by my family, but must we accept that practice to govern our life for all times? That is not for me.'

Bandana replied, 'One cannot demolish faith by argument, but neither can I give you any assurance of happiness. I have no knowledge of the person who holds the key to such a guarantee. I have watched many prenuptial heart-warming courtships, but I have also seen breakups when that early attraction evaporated into nothingness. Do not fall into that trap, Dijubabu. Do not chase an illusory golden deer.'

'This means that Sudhirbabu has ravaged your heart pretty badly.'

Bandana smiled, 'Yes. You also contributed to that, and now it is Ashok's turn. For all my ill luck, if he lasts, it will not be such a bad thing.'

'What is your problem with Ashok?'

'Just this. He is falling in love with me.'

'Are you firmly resolved that no one must come anywhere near falling in love with you?'

'Yes, it is my resolve. I do not wish to step into colossal trouble in anticipation of the immense happiness of marriage. I have warned Ashok that I will run away from him if he falls in love with me.'

'And what did he say to that?'

'Nothing, he just stared at me. I felt sorry for him.'

'If you are truly sorry, then there is still some hope. All this is nothing but a reaction of staying at your masi's house—a passing phase.'

'That may be. It is not impossible. But I have certainly learnt a lot. Had I not visited Kolkata, I would have been unaware of so many things!'

After being quiet for some time, Dwijadas said, 'We don't have much time now. Let me have your last piece of advice—what should I do?'

Bandana teased him, 'You want my advice? Truly?'

'Yes, truly. I am not like my dada. I need friends, I need counselling. You asked me to get married. I will do so. But if I have no love and no friends, how can I carry out the responsibilities you have charged me with?'

His anxiety bothered Bandana. She said, 'Have no fear, Dijubabu. God will provide you with friends when you are truly in need. Keep faith.'

Dwijadas was about to say something when he heard Maitreyee's voice outside. 'Are you there, Dijubabu? Ma wants to see you.'

Dwijadas stood up and said, 'Your train leaves at midnight. I will call on you at half past eleven.' He left the room.

TWENTY-FIVE

In a delayed response to the news of Bandana's safe arrival in Bombay, Dwijadas wrote that he had not been able to write to her earlier as he had been preoccupied with work. Everything was as Bandana had seen when she left. There was nothing new to share with her. Maitreyee's father had gone back to Calcutta, but she was still there. She had been taking great care of Mother and also running the home very well. Everyone at home was pleased with her, and Dwijadas had no difficulty with her.

Three months had passed since that letter, with no further communication either way. Bandana was anxious to hear about Bipradas, her mejdi, and Basu, but could not figure out a way to find out about them. They had not informed her about how they were, or indeed, where they were. Though she desperately wanted to, she was too embarrassed to write to Dwijadas for information. Slowly, the acute memory of Balarampur as well as the associated pain and anguish abated. With every passing day, as she regained tranquility, she also began to realize that their relationship was not based on any real bond. She appreciated that she had no role to play in that old, orthodox, ritual-bound family, nor could she ever be intimate with them. Their disparate education and culture had created a disconnect that was both absolute and inflexible.

Meanwhile, Bandana's masi arrived in Bombay, apparently on grounds of health. Oddly enough, a doctor in Punjab, where she lived, had advised her that the climate in Bombay was more salubrious than in Punjab. She nursed a grievance against Bandana because she had not called on her before returning to Bombay; however, being aware of Bandana's temperament, she dared not complain openly to Raysahib. But she threw a hint one day at dinner when she observed, 'I do not know if it has occurred to you, but from my experience, I have found that a single child, boy or girl, grows up so self-willed that one has difficulty in getting along with them.'

Raysahib readily agreed, as he had a specimen very near at hand. Happily citing it, he said, 'Just like my little girl. If she says no, no one can make her say otherwise. I have been observing her since she was a toddler.'

Bandana said to her father, 'Is that why you do not love your disobedient daughter any longer?'

Raysahib protested vigorously, 'What? You a disobedient child? Never! No one can say that.'

Bandana laughed, 'But you said that just now.'

'Me? Never.'

Masi joined in the laughter.

'Tell me, Father, was it that my mother could not stand me either?'

Raysahib said, 'Your mother? The number of fights we had over you! When you were a little child, you broke my watch once, and your mother was very angry and boxed your ears. You ran to me sobbing, and I picked you up in my arms. That day, I did not speak to your mother at all.' Moved emotionally by surging old memories, he drew her close to him and fondled her head.

Bandana asked, 'Why are you not as fond of me as you were when I was a child?'

Raysahib appealed to Masi, 'Just listen to her, Mrs Ghosal.'

Bandana complained, 'Why do you then tell me all the time that you will feel relieved after marrying me off? Have I become an eyesore?'

'Mrs Ghosal, did you hear what she said?'

Masi said, 'But truly Bandana, you won't be able to understand the anxiety of parents when their daughters grow up. You will only understand this when you have a daughter.'

'I do not want to understand, Masi.'

'Do understand, child, that a father has his responsibility. Parents are not immortals. They will be at fault if they fail to think about their children's future. Only other parents can apprehend your father's worries. I hardly had any peace until I got Prakriti married. You would not know how many sleepless nights I went through, but your father will. Had your mother been alive, she would also be facing the same situation.'

Raysahib nodded his head, 'True, very true.'

Masi continued to talk to him, 'Had her mother been living today, she would have kept after you about Bandana. I did the same to my husband. Looking back now, I feel ashamed.'

Raysahib agreed, 'You were not at fault. It is always so.'

Masi continued, 'That is how I feel. We are getting old and do not know how long we will live. If we cannot get our daughters settled while we are still on earth, I shudder to think about their future. My husband was sick with worry.'

Bandana could not stand it any longer. She noticed that her father was getting increasingly shaken and had also stopped eating. She was upset at her masi. 'You had uselessly scared Uncle in so many ways, and now trying to do the same to my father. Why must you do that? Father has many years of life yet, and he will do what is good for his daughter. Do not nag him.'

Masi was not the one to give up, particularly when Bandana's father endorsed what she said. He said, 'Your masi is right, Bandana. I really do not keep all that well. In any case, she is our relation, and if she does not warn us in time, who will?' Masi noticed that Bandana's face was clouded. Embarrassed, she said, 'No, Mr Ray, you must not say that. We all pray that you live for a hundred years. All I wanted to say...'

Raysahib stopped her, 'You are quite right. Truly, I do not keep all that well. One ought to be mindful while one still has time. It will be wrong of me if I neglect my obligations.'

Suppressing her displeasure, Bandana said, 'Masi, it looks like Father's appetite is ruined for now.'

Masi quickly retreated, 'Let us stop this conversation. I will be very upset if you do not eat properly.'

Raysahib had really lost his appetite, but he forced himself to pick at some food. He asked later, 'How is your son-in-law's practice progressing?'

'He has just started. But it is not going badly from what I am told.' Swallowing a mouthful of food, Masi continued,

'Regardless of how his practice progresses, that is not the major aspect of life according to me. Far more important is his character. Unless that is untarnished, no woman can really be happy.'

'Unquestionably,' agreed Raysahib.

Masi continued, 'My outlook is based on the way in which I have been brought up and educated in my natal family. An iota less from that standard is not acceptable to me. When I see Ashok, my mind goes back to the moral ambience that prevailed in our family, the ambience in which I grew up. Ashok is moulded in the same cast as my father and his elder brother— simple, generous, and of strong moral fibre.'

Raysahib agreed and said, 'That was my impression too. Very honest. I was charmed by him during his brief stay here.' Then, turning to his daughter, he asked, 'Don't you agree? We liked him a great deal, did we not? I felt sad the day he left.'

Bandana agreed, 'Yes, Father, a very nice man indeed; as polite as he is gentle. I would have been in great trouble had he not accompanied me to Bombay.'

Masi said, 'You may have noticed that there is no trace of snobbery in him. Sadly, that is not true for many amongst us.'

Bandana laughed, 'I cannot recall seeing any snobs at your place.'

Masi also laughed, 'Of course, you must have. How can they fool such a clever girl like you?'

It made Raysahib very happy. He cheerfully added, 'It is rare to come across so intelligent a person. I know it sounds like a fond father's boast. Nonetheless, it is the truth.'

Bandana said, 'For heaven's sake, Masi, drop this topic, or else you will not be able to hold Father in check. Earlier, you carped about the obstinacy of an only child, but you do not know of the conceit of the father of a sole daughter. According to my father, there is no one in this world like his daughter.'

Masi said, 'I too am guilty of that belief, Bandana. Punish me then, too, if you must.'

With a smile of deep satisfaction, her father said, 'I do not know if I am conceited, but I know that I am most fortunate in having such a precious daughter. Very few fathers are so blessed.'

Bandana nudged him, 'Father, you did not touch the sandesh at all. Is it not good?'

Raysahib broke a piece of the sandesh and ate it. He declared, 'Everything is made by Bandana herself. After coming back from Calcutta, she has changed our daily diet and replaced it with Bengali cuisine. I do not know who told her, but she hardly allows meat to be served. Says that it is not suitable for my health. These Bengali dishes suit me well in my growing age. My appetite has improved.'

Bandana said, 'Masi is not used to this kind of food. She must be having trouble with her meal.'

Masi ignored the slight ridicule in Bandana's voice and quickly said, 'I have no problem, I quite like this kind of food. The change of air is not the only thing that will help me; a change of diet is equally important. Perhaps, my health has improved rapidly because of this.'

'So you feel better, Masi?'

'Yes, I do, indeed.'

'In that case, why not stay a little longer? Restore your health fully.'

'Sadly, I cannot. Ashok writes that he intends to visit Punjab by the end of this month for a change of air, so I need to be back before then.'

Lunch was almost over, and Raysahib was about to leave the table. It made Masi anxious. She had prepared a favourable ground for what she was planning to propose, and if she let the opportunity pass, it could be difficult to find another. Overcoming her diffidence, she said, 'Mr Ray, I wish to talk to you if you are free now...'

Raysahib sat down. 'Yes, you can talk to me now.'

Masi said, 'I believe that Bandana is not unwilling. It is true that Ashok is not well off, but by dint of his education and the strength of his character, he is sure to rise in life. If you do not consider him unfit for your daughter...'

Raysahib was taken by surprise. He said, 'But how can this marriage be possible? He is your nephew. So, in a way, they are cousins.'

Masi said, 'But that is only in name, otherwise the relationship is very remote. It just happens that my grandmother and Bandana's mother's grandmother were sisters, and that makes me Bandana's masi. This marriage is not prohibited.'

Raysahib thought it over. He said, 'From the little I have seen of Ashok and from whatever I have heard from Bandana, I do not regard him as unfit. I will have to marry her off some day, but before that I must know her mind.'

Masi lovingly coaxed Bandana to speak her mind, 'Don't feel shy in front of your father. Tell your father what you wish for.'

Bandana's face turned red for an instant, and then she enunciated very firmly, 'I have abandoned my wish, so there is no need to probe into it.'

Raysahib was alarmed. 'What does this mean?'

Bandana replied, 'I do not know if I can really explain to you what I mean, but do not think that I will go against you. When Satididi got married, she was only nine years old, but she accepted her husband selected by her parents. It was not her own choice. But thanks to her good fortune, her husband turned out to be a rare personality. And I will do the same. I will trust my fate. Before I left, Bipradasbabu, who is a very saintly person, gave me his blessings and assured me that God would put me in the place that was best for me. His words will never be wrong. I will do exactly what you ask me to do—without hesitation or fear.'

Raysahib looked at her bewildered, but said nothing.

Masi said, 'Your mejdi was nothing but a child when she got married, so there was no question about her views. But you are an adult now. Your life is in your hands, and it does not seem right that you will leave it to your destiny with your eyes shut.'

'I do not know about that. But, like her, I will accept my fate.'

'How can your father make a decision if you talk so disinterestedly?'

'The way his elder brother did about Satididi, the way his earlier generations got their children married, let my father follow that tradition for my marriage.'

'And you will remain indifferent and not look around for yourself or give it any thought?'

'I have looked around and I have thought a great deal, but I will not do so any more. I will now wholly depend on my father's blessings and my destiny.'

Masi spoke bitterly, 'We all accept destiny, but I can't believe that you would abandon your education, society, and culture and become so influenced by your limited association with the Mukhujye family. From your words, it is hard to believe that you are our old Bandana. It seems as if you have moved away from us and are no longer our own.'

Bandana said, 'No Masi, I have not moved away. I know that I will not have to make strangers of my people in order to make the Mukhujyes my own. Do not fret about me.'

Masi asked, 'May I then send a telegram asking Ashok to come here?'

'If you wish to,' said Bandana and left the room.

'Mr Ray, shall I send a telegram in your name?' As she said it, Masi looked up and found tears in Raysahib's eyes. She could not understand the reason for it. When he asked not to send the telegram immediately, she was at a loss and said, 'Why not, Mr Ray? Bandana gave her consent.'

'No, not today,' he said, and fell silent. The silence and the tears in his eyes annoyed Masi. Such sentimentality in someone of his age and status irritated her. But she could not insist.

Raysahib said, 'As a father, I have thought about it. But she has no mother, and I have to take her place. So I need time.'

Masi considered such feelings stupid. Whether Raysahib guessed it or not, he spoke with a forced smile, 'The problem is that we cannot properly follow what she says. This is true not just of today, but I have noticed it since her return from Bengal. She did give her consent, but was it she or was it her new-found religion? That is what I cannot fathom.'

'What do you mean by her new-found religion?'

'Frankly, I do not know. But I have the impression that she returned from Bengal imbued with some ideas that now pervade her life. She seems to have altered her pattern of life in every way—her food habits, the way she talks, her movements—nothing is like her earlier self. After her early morning bath, she comes everyday to my room and touches my feet. I told her, "But you never did this before." To which she said, "I did not know all this then, Father. Now that I start the day having touched your feet, I have the feeling that it protects me the whole day."' As Raysahib related it, his eyes filled with tears again.

Masi was decidedly irritated when she heard it. She said, 'Bandana absorbed all these ideas from the Mukhujye family. You know how rigid they are. But this is not any religion; it is nothing but a load of superstition. Does she do puja as well?'

Raysahib said, 'I have no idea. Perhaps, she does not. I also accepted all this as superstition and I tried to restrain her. But she does not argue any longer as she used to before. She just keeps quiet, and that effectively shuts me up. I can't tell her anything.'

Masi retaliated, 'But this is weakness on your part. Know for sure that it is not religion, but superstition. To encourage her in this is wrong, perhaps even a crime.'

Raysahib spoke hesitantly, 'May be so. We just talk about religion, but never bother about it, so I have no clue to its nature. Yet, I wonder who wrought such a radical transformation in my daughter? Where has her laughter and the spirit of joy gone? I tell her, "Little one, please do not hide anything from your father. I trust that nothing is wrong with your health?" And she laughs and says, "No, Father, I am fine. I am not unwell." She then goes back to her work, but it breaks my heart. She is our only child, and I raised her all by myself. I would give my entire fortune away if I just could get my old Bandana back...'

Masi said forcefully, 'You will get her back, believe me. It is nothing but a passing feeling of despondency. There could also be a touch of religious fervour, but that hardly matters. It is likely to be a fleeting phase, resulting from her association with that family. Get her married and everything will be normal shortly. A lifetime of education stays for a lifetime, Mr Ray, fads are short-lived.'

Raysahib was reassured, but not really convinced. He said, 'I do not know the source of her inspiration, but I have been told that if the source is truly a great person, this inspiration becomes a permanent feature, which then alters one's life's training in no time. It gets into the bloodstream and becomes a part of one's life. And that is my fear.'

Masi was openly contemptuous. She said, 'Absolute garbage! I have seen many such cases in my life, but all these are impermanent. It will become normal again. Nevertheless, we must be careful not to let it continue. Please send a telegram to Ashok now asking him to come here.'

'Today?'

'Yes, today, and in your name.'

Raysahib gave his consent willy-nilly, 'Do whatever you think is right. Ashok is a fine boy of good manners, or else Bandana would not have agreed to travel to Bombay with him.'

Masi was keen to expand on that topic, but could not. Bandana walked in to tell her father, 'I have been invited to tea by the daughters of Haji Sahib. I will go in the afternoon, but please pick me up on your way back from office.'

Masi asked, 'But you will not eat anything in their house, will you Bandana?'

'No, Masi.'

'Why not?' asked her father.

'Because I don't feel like it. Father, you won't forget, right?'

'Forget to pick you up? How can I?' He laughed a little and then said, 'Ashok will be here. I am going to send him a telegram today.'

'Fair enough, Father.'

Masi reminded her, 'It is on my insistence that he will be here. Please do see that he is treated with respect here.'

'We do not disrespect our guests, Masi. Ashokbabu knows that well.'

Pleased with Bandana's reply, Raysahib said, 'I will send the telegram on my way to the office. It is Friday today, so he should be here by Monday if there is no problem.'

The watchman brought in the mail, consisting in the main of newspapers from various places and some letters. Of late, Bandana had shown little interest in the mail as she knew that it was futile to expect letters everyday. She also had hardly anybody who would write to her. She was about to leave when Raysahib called her back and said, 'You have two letters. There is one for you as well, Mrs Ghosal.'

Masi apparently took more interest in other people's letters than her own. Craning her neck to look at Bandana's letters, she commented, 'I can see that one is from Ashok. From whom is the other one?'

Bandana ignored the unnecessary curiosity and, picking up her two letters, went to her room.

Raysahib said with a little smile, 'She corresponds with Ashok, I see. I will send him a telegram. Let him come here.'

Masi flashed a smile of satisfaction, hinting that she knew more about them.

Raysahib returned in the evening alone from Haji Sahib's place. Bandana had not visited them. Masi said with a long face that Bandana had not come out of her room since she had gone in with her letters.

He asked anxiously, 'Did she have nothing to eat?'

'No, nothing after the fruits she had at breakfast.'

Raysahib hastened to his daughter's room. He was shocked when he saw her face. 'What is the trouble?'

Bandana said, 'Father, I have to travel to Balarampur by tonight's train.'

'Balarampur? But why?'

'I received a letter from Dijubabu. Will you read it?'

'Better read it to me, I will listen to you.' He sat down on a chair. Bandana stood close to him reading the letter, which went like this—

Dear Respected Lady,

I remember the day you left. You asked me to keep you informed from time to time. I said I was rather too lazy to do so and not good at writing letters. Please ask someone else to do it.

You appeared amazed by what I said, went back to your car, and did not ask me again. Perhaps, you thought that what one could say to a person who was so discourteous.

Yes, I am like that. I only hoped that if I had to write to you, it would be on a major issue. And may this letter atone for all my failings.

I used to think, is there only unexpected misery for humans in life? Is there no unexpected happiness?

Will Dada's adored deity keep his eyes shut and never open them to see what is happening? Must catastrophes last forever? And will there be no one to shake them up? There is no such power. Neither did God yield, nor His devotee. And yet, the lamp continues to burn with an eternal and steady flame.

Let me make clear why I write this way. Three days ago, Dada returned home with only Basu. No one else. Basu had no shoes, and a white scarf was tied around his neck. I was up on the roof sunning myself. A darkness descended in front of my eyes— like a moonless night. After a few minutes, I saw clearly again. I had never experienced this before.

I met Dada when I went down. He told me, 'Your boudie passed away yesterday morning. I do not have much money, so please arrange for her last rites as modestly as possible. Where is Ma?'

'In Dhaka, with her daughter.'

'In Dhaka? She might not be able to come then. Get Basu write to her about his mother.'

I said, 'Yes, he will.'

Basu came running to me, put his arms round my neck, and buried his face on my chest. Then he broke down and kept crying. That crying had no language, just as I have no language to describe it in this letter. I picked him up and ran to my room. He continued to cry with his face resting on my chest. I told myself, 'Dear Basu, your loss is colossal, but someone else's sense of loss transcends yours. You will have people crowding around you and offer you consolation, but that other will have none. The only hope is if Bandana can understand.'

I do not know how much time passed. Finally, I dried his eyes and told him, 'Be brave. You may not have your mother or father, but I am here. I may never be able to repay my debts to them, but will never deny them either. At this moment of our most grievous loss and distress, this is your uncle's promise to you.'

There is no point in lingering on this topic. There is nothing more to say. When I was a boy, Father used to call me foolhardy, Mother called me ill-mannered, and on several occasions, Dada would be annoyed with me. Feeling neglected and without love, living in this house sometimes got poisonous for me. Then Boudie would come to me and ask, 'What is it that you want, Thakurpo?' And I would reply angrily, 'I don't want anything, I want to get away from here.'

'And when do you propose to go?'

'Today.'

She would laugh and say, 'You don't have my permission to go. Try to do that against my will!'

I could not leave, but she did. Are permissions only denied to me? Was there no one to deny her permission to leave?

I asked Dada, 'What happened?' He said, 'Perhaps, she was not all that well when we left. She appeared to have something on her mind. I took her to Haridwar where she fell sick. Then I took her to Kashi and she died there.'

I asked, 'Did she receive proper medical attention?' He said, 'To the extent possible.' And only Dada knows what this 'extent' was.

I thought of asking him—why did you punish me in this way? What had I done? But looking at him, I did not have the strength to say this. I asked, 'Did she leave a message for anyone?'

He replied, 'She was conscious up to ten hours before her death. I asked her if she had any message for Ma.

'She said, "No."

'"For me?"

'"No."

'"For Diju?"

'"Yes, give him my blessings and tell him that he has got everything."'

I ran to Boudie's empty room. She had always been shy of being photographed. There was only one in her cupboard, a photograph taken by me. I stood facing her picture and said, 'I am blessed, Boudie, and I now know your command. I never thought you would leave us so soon; but if you can see, you will know that I have not ignored your orders. Just give me this strength that, bereaved of you, I will not openly shed tears.' That is all about Boudie for now.

Let me talk about myself now. Before you left, you had asked me to get married because the load of all the responsibilities would be too much for me, and so I needed someone to share it with me. You had in mind that Maitreyee should be that someone. I did not resist then, because having lost 99 per cent of my life's purpose, there did not seem to be any point in arguing about a mere 1 per cent.

But that is also gone. Boudie's death has created an insurmountable barrier. What is this barrier? Maitreyee can assume responsibility, but she is incapable of carrying this burden; and, to me, it is this burden that appears very heavy. I must admit that during our difficult days, she did a great deal for us. I am extremely grateful to her, and will never forget it.

Late last night, Basu woke up and started crying. I managed to put him back to sleep and then went to see Dada. I saw him deeply engrossed in a book. 'What are you reading, Dada?' I asked. Closing the book, he smiled and asked, 'Tell me, what brings you here?' I could not tell him what I intended to. What does it matter to Bipradas if Basu cried in his sleep? I asked him, 'Where will you be after the shraddha is over? In Calcutta?'

He said, 'No, I will be away on pilgrimage.'

'And when will you be back?'

'I will not.'

Stunned, I stared at him. I did not have the slightest doubt that his resolution was inflexible. He was renouncing his life.

But to whom could I go to weeping and pleading? To this stony-hearted ascetic?

'What about Basu?' I asked.

He said, 'I have located an ashram in the Himalayas which takes in young boys. They look after them and educate them as well.'

'You propose to put him in the hands of those people? Though it was I who have nurtured him?'

I did not wait for his reply. I ran back to my room. Sitting next to Basu, I thought deeply all night. I had no clue where it would all end. And then, I thought of you. You told me that when I really needed a friend, God would bring one to my doorstep. You had asked me to believe that. I do not know who this friend is and

*when that person will come to me. But I still believe that in my
hour of need, my friend will be there.*

Dwijadas

Tears were flowing from Raysahib's eyes when the letter was
being read. He said, 'Yes, go there today. I will not stop you.
Take our watchman and old Himu with you.'

Bandana bent down to touch his feet and said, 'I will make
the arrangements for my trip.'

TWENTY-SIX

Biraj Datta, the manager, was at the railway station to meet her and escorted her to the car.

Bandana asked, 'Has Ma arrived yet?'

'No, Didi.'

'Maitreyee?'

'No, no one has gone to fetch her.'

'How is Basu?'

'He is fine.'

'Mukhujyemashai? Dijubabu?'

'Barababu is fine, but Chhotobabu does not look so well.'

'Does he have a temperature?' Bandana asked.

Datta said, 'I really do not know, Didi, but he is carrying on with all his responsibilities.'

After a brief silence, Bandana said, 'I have a feeling that Ma is unlikely to return during this difficult time. Despite the sadness, the shraddha has to be observed. Is anything being done about that?'

'Yes, certainly. It is being arranged on the same scale as it was for the late Kartababu.'

Not being able to follow it, she asked, 'Like whom? Like the shraddha ceremony of Mukhujyemashai's father? On such a large scale?'

Datta replied, 'Yes, almost. You will see for yourself. Barababu told, "Diju, don't go overboard. There must be a limit to everything." Chhotobabu said, "I am aware that there are limits, but the limits are not the same for everyone." Barababu laughed and said, "But Diju, you are crossing the limits for everyone." Chhotobabu said, "In that case, forgive me this time. I can cross any limit, but I cannot undermine my boudie's dignity."'

Datta added, 'They talked no more, but please see if you can do anything about this. The expenses will come to between twenty and twenty-five thousand.'

'And all to Chhotobabu's account?'

'That is so.'

Bandana asked, 'Do you think that is a very large sum for him to bear?'

Biraj Datta said, 'It may not be, but recently a great deal of money was spent. It is time to be careful. And who knows when a new crisis strikes us.'

'What new crisis?'

'Have you not heard about the legal tangle with Sasadharbabu? Regardless of the final verdict, the consequences can be damaging.'

'Why did you not stop him?'

'Stop him? He is not like our Barababu that he will pay heed to us. There was only one person who could check him, and she has now gone to heaven.'

On reaching the house, Bandana found heaps of firewood stacked on one side of the field that faced the house. The huts that had been created on the occasion of Dayamoyee's religious function were being repaired. A large dais was being built by an army of workmen. Datta had not exaggerated.

Alighting from the car, Bandana headed straight for Dwijadas's room. He was resting on his bed, leaning on a big bolster. At the sound of the shifting of curtains, he sat up and said, 'So, my friend is here on her own right at my doorsteps.'

Bandana said, 'Yes, she has, but why are you in bed betimes?'

Dwijadas said, 'I was thinking of you with my eyes shut, telling you in my mind that Bandana, there is no end to my misery. My body is frail, my heart has lost all hope. I don't think I can push along any more. My boat will go down midstream; and there is no way can I cross over to the other side.'

Bandana said, 'You have to. I will let you off now and take over the plying of your boat.'

'Please do that, but do not abandon me in a fit of rage.'

Bandana went to him, bent down, and touched his feet. She had never done so before. When she stood up, both their eyes welled up with tears. Bandana said, 'I never knew that your eyes could also get teary.'

Dwijadas said, 'Neither did I. Perhaps, the passage was choked for far too long. The very first time it opened was the day you left, asking me to leave everything in Maitreyee's hands. I dried my eyes and told myself that I would not ask for anything from someone who could hurt me so easily. But that was not to be. Boudie suddenly died, Ma left to be with her daughter as soon as we got involved in a court case with Sasadhar, and Dada told me of his resolution to quit this worldly life—as it were, in an instant, my whole world was demolished in an earthquake. I could accept all this. But when I heard that Basu was to be dispatched to an unknown ashram, it was unacceptable. For once, I contemplated getting away from all of this, leaving whatever remains to Kalyani's sons. It was then that I recalled what you told me before you left—you had asked me to keep faith that a friend would come to me when I direly need that friend. This was my last such need, and so I wrote to you. I jettisoned my doubts and told myself that my friend will come. Otherwise, you would be proved wrong, and so would my boudie's final wishes for me. With what strength can I bear the responsibilities that she left behind?' As he spoke, tears rolled down his eyes.

Bandana said, 'It is a common belief that you are very insubordinate—you paid no heed to anybody with the sole exception of your boudie.'

Dwijadas said, 'That is your fear, I see. Had Boudie been alive, she could have provided you with an answer.' He dried his eyes.

Bandana said, 'I have my answer. I have no fear now.' She took Dwijadas's hand in hers, mused for sometime, and said, 'You are not the only one to have come through an earthquake. I am also a victim of a severe tremor. I had lost everything, but I have won back that which is indestructible and unshakeable. Let me go and meet Dada. The day I left, he blessed me with the wish, "Bandana, may my blessings bring to you the one who is your own." I had total faith in the words of that saintly person.

I knew for certain that it was true. What I did not know was that the blessing will bring my own to me in the midst of such unhappy times.'

'Diju, has Bandana come?' asked Annada as she walked in.

'Yes, Anudi, I am here.' She turned round and was shocked by Annada's grief-stricken look. Resting her head on her chest, she said, 'Anudi, I could have never have imagined that I would live to see you like this.' She broke into tears as did Annada, who tenderly ran her palm on Bandana's back and spoke softly, 'Do not please leave abruptly any more. Stay on for some days. What more can I say?'

Bandana said nothing. With her face still buried in Annada's breast, she nodded. Later, she lifted her face, wiped her eyes, and asked, 'Where is Basu?'

'The servants have taken him to give him a bath.'

'Who cooks for him?'

Annada said, 'Diju does. They eat together. Basu sleeps on his bed.' Tears started flowing once again. She wiped her eyes dry and said, 'It is not only that Basu has lost his mother; Diju too has lost his. Everyone has been asking that what is the point of such a big ritual for the death of a young housewife who died prematurely? They try to desist; they see it as an unnecessary showing off. But they do not know that in a previous birth, she was his mother. How can he accept any affront to her dignity?'

Pointing to Bandana, Dwijadas said, 'I have no worry now that Bandana is here. I will unload all my responsibilities on her and move to the side.'

Annada asked, 'How can an outsider—a girl from another family—assume such responsibilities?'

'But Anudi, they are the ones who take on the load and carry them out. I told her that I can no longer bear the burden of this sorrow. If, on top of that, Basu is sent away, I will say that I do not care about the Mukhujye clan of Balarampur or their image built up over generations. I will leave everything to Sasadhar's sons and abdicate this life. Diju is also capable of this sacrifice, not just Dada. I may not opt for the life of an ascetic— I do not understand it, but I can easily renounce my wealth and walk away.'

Annada took hold of Bandana's hands and pleaded, 'Can you not persuade Bipin to change his mind and keep Basu here?'

'Yes, I can.'

'And this ruinous lawsuit against the son-in-law? Can you not prevent it?'

'Yes, that also. I have agreed to come into this family as the younger daughter-in-law on the condition that he will never go against my wishes.'

Annada did not quite follow the significance of what Bandana said. Bandana continued, 'What is lost is lost, but do we have to lose Mother at the same time? How can I bring her back if I cannot stop this lawsuit?'

Taking a bunch of keys out from under his pillow, Dwijadas dropped it at Bandana's feet. He said, 'Take it. I will never go against you, this is my promise to you.'

Bandana picked it up and tied it to the end of her sari.

Everything was clear to Annada. She drew Bandana close to her and tears rolled down her face.

***

Bandana went to Bipradas's room. Touching his feet, she said, 'Barda, I am back.'

He registered that new form of address, but ignoring it, he said, 'I knew from your father's telegram that you were coming. I trust that you had a comfortable journey.'

'Yes.'

'And who escorted you?'

'Our watchman and our old retainer Himu.'

'And your father, is he well?'

'He is.'

'Have you noticed Diju's madness?'

Bandana asked, 'Are you referring to the arrangements for the shraddha? Why do you call it madness? It is only right that it be done on a scale befitting her.'

'How can he manage all this, Bandana?'

'If he cannot, I can.'

Bipradas said, 'I know your capability, but the trouble is the frame of your mind. We will all be relieved if you do not desert us abruptly.'

Bandana said, 'I was a stranger then, but I am now here as the younger daughter-in-law of this house. If I have reasons to be annoyed, I will be annoyed, but how can I walk out now? That road is closed to me.' She showed the bunch of keys to Bipradas. 'These are the keys to the safes and lockers. I am now in charge.'

A sense of happiness and disbelief overtook Bipradas. Bandana went on, 'I have no inhibitions to speak to you; nothing to hide either. Just as a mortal person does not hide anything from God. Do you recall your benediction on the day I left? You assured me that I would find the person who would really be my own. From that day onwards, I have calmly contemplated that the person who is above all vices, who is sacred from birth, and who speaks only the truth has given me his blessings. So I knew I had nothing to fear. I would certainly find him who would be my husband.' Her eyes filled with tears.

Bipradas went to her and silently blessed her once again. This time, Bandana placed her head on Bipradas's feet. When she got up, Bipradas told her, 'Let me tell you, Bandana, there is no one rarer than the one you have found today. Remember these words of mine all your life.'

'Yes, Barda, I will. I will never forget it even for a day.'

She was quiet for a little while and then spoke, 'When I nursed you in your illness, you had wished to reward me. I did not ask for anything then. Do you recall this?'

'Yes, I do.'

'I want that reward now. I want Basu.'

Bipradas said smilingly, 'Take him.'

'I will teach him to call me Ma.'

'Do that. Be both his father and mother. And, of course, I am leaving you with the responsibility of guarding the great tradition of the Mukhujye family.'

Bandana accepted the responsibility and said, 'I have just one request. When I did not know myself, I once offended you gravely. I know my mistake now and ask you to forgive me.'

'I forgave that a long time ago. I knew you would find the one you wanted from the depth of your heart. You have nothing to be ashamed of.' Bandana's eyes had started watering again, but she checked it and said, 'Just one more request. Will you not stay with us even for a day? I have never been able to take care of you to my heart's content. There are now no barriers, and neither am I embarassed or ashamed. Please stay with me for a few more days. Give me the opportunity to worship you with my care.' She looked at him with eyes filled with tears—her plea seemed to emerge straight from her heart.

Bipradas smiled at her.

Bandana said, 'It is this smiling silence of yours that I dread the most. How steely is your heart! It neither melts nor sways. Will you not give me an answer?'

Bipradas then broke into laughter. Tender, loving, transparent. Bandana had never seen him laugh like that. She said, 'Yes, I have your answer, I will not press you further. But please tell me how to find peace of mind—the mind that cannot stop shedding tears.'

Bipradas consoled her, 'You will find it on the day you understand that your dada did not leave home to plunge into the depths of misery. Not before then.'

'How will I know this?'

'Only by having faith in me. You know, do you not, that I never lie?'

Bandana, after a deep sigh, said, 'Yes, I accept that. From now on, I will try to convince myself with all my heart that Dada is right. He is wedded to the truth; he cannot assuage my mind by untruths. He is gone in search of that holy place where lies man's ultimate bliss.'

Bipradas said, 'Yes, do that. Convince your mind that Dada has gone in search of the path which leads to the ultimate in elegance, in principle, and in splendour. He should not be stopped, nor be called misguided; and it will be wrong to mourn for him.'

Bandana's eyes once again filled with tears. She said, 'That will be so. If I do not see him again in my life, I will still believe that he was not wrong and it will be improper to mourn for him.'

Peeping through the curtain, Biraj Datta said, 'Didi, there is an urgent matter. We need you.'

'Please wait, I will be with you. Dada, I have to leave now.'

***

The shraddha ceremony for Sati was performed with splendour. Everyone agreed that it was conducted in keeping with the normal standard of the Mukhujye family; there was no discrimination between the ritual for the elderly and the young.

After her bath in the morning, when Bandana went to Bipradas's room, she was amazed to see Dayamoyee sitting next to him. She had arrived by the early morning train, unknown to anyone. Bandana was shocked by her look. Her once fair complexion had turned dark, her short hair was rough, she was covered with dust, her eyes sunken, and her forehead was lined—Bandana had not seen such poignant appearance afflicted by grief and pain. She recalled her earlier image, not so long ago, when she reigned there as Bipradas's mother—powerful and gracious. All her glory seemed to have been ground to the dust.

Bandana touched her feet and asked, 'When did you come, Ma? I did not know.'

Dayamoyee embraced her and said, 'Who is now bothered about me? Earlier, I would arrive as the mother of Bipradas, and so everyone, man and boy, knew about my return. Bipin, the shraddha affair is over now. Why don't the two of us, mother and son, leave today?'

Bipradas smiled and replied, 'Not immediately, Mother. There is nothing to stop the mother–son duo from going away, but not today. Bandana's father is arriving tomorrow and, anyway, how can you leave now before handing over the responsibilities of this home to your younger daughter-in-law?'

It silenced Dayamoyee, briefly though. Recovering, she said, 'Yes, so be it. I cannot say that I don't accept this. That will not be true. Anyway, the wait will be short.'

'Only a week, Ma. On this day next week, we will set out on our journey.'

Bandana said, 'Ma, please let me take to your room.'

Dayamoyee declined, shaking her head, 'I am sorry, but I must disappoint you. I will remain in this room for the few days I am here, and the two of us set out from this room the day we leave. All that is inside the house is now yours.'

Bandana did not insist and, touching her feet once again, she left the room.

On receiving Bipradas's letter, Raysahib came to Balarampur with seven days' leave. After giving his daughter's hand in marriage to Diju, he returned to Bombay.

The marriage was shorn of the usual frills—there was no shehnai music; no press of guests; ululations were muted. It was a subdued affair.

When they were alone in their room, Bandana looked at Dwijadas's dejected face and asked, 'Tell me, what is it you are thinking of?'

Dwijadas said, 'You. I am thinking how remarkable you are.'

'Why?'

'Otherwise, you could not have done what you have done for me. Just to rescue us from a disaster, you came to me after a long walk along a distressful path.'

Bandana asked, 'Would you have not done the same?'

'No.'

Bandana said, 'I don't believe you. Do you know what was in my mind? As I placed the garland around your neck, I asked myself what good deeds I could have done to have been rewarded with a husband like you, and to have found Basu, Ma, and Baradada. And to have received the responsibility of this huge house. But do you know what is due to a woman from our society?'

'No,' Dwijadas said.

Bandana stopped in her tracks and then said, 'On this day of my supreme good fortune and happiness, I rather not cast aspertions on the less fortunate. That would be improper.'

Dwijadas said, 'It will not be improper. Please say it.'

She said, 'You are tired. Go to sleep. Let me massage your head.'

A little later, she said, 'I was thinking of Mejdi. When she decided to go with Baradada, I said to her, "You are not a party to this dispute, so why are you going?" She told me, "Where a husband has no place, neither has the wife. Not even for a day." She told me that I would have appreciated this were I married. I did not follow her then, but I realize today that I cannot stay anywhere if you are not there.'

She paused for some time and then said, 'It is just a few hours ago that I chanted the mantras with the priest, but it seems to me that each drop of my blood has completely transformed.'

Dwijadas opened his eyes and looked at her, and then taking her hands, he put them on his chest and, without any words, closed his eyes again.

***

Sunday arrived. The day Dayamoyee and Bipradas were to set off on their journey. People had heard that Dayamoyee's pilgrimage would be over some day and the pull of her family would bring her back home. But Bipradas's journey would never end and he will never be back. A car was waiting outside. Everyone from the house as well as from neighbouring houses were there. Women stood on the second-floor verandah, shedding tears. Before stepping into the car, Bipradas asked, 'I don't see Diju. Where is he?'

Someone told him, 'He has gone out on some work.' Bipradas smiled and said, 'He has run away. All his bravado is for show; in fact, he is the coward of the cowards.'

Basu was there, holding Bandana's hand. He asked, 'Father, when will you be back? Come soon.'

Bipradas affectionately tousled his hair, but gave him no answer. Bandana touched her mother-in-law's feet. She told Bandana, 'Basu will be here with you, as well as your family deity Radhagovindaji. If and when I come back, I will take them over from you.' She stemmed her surging tears.

Bandana first greeted Bipradas from a distance and then, going close to him, she spoke in an emotional voice, 'One day, I saw you deep in meditation in your puja room in Calcutta, and I see the same image today. I have no sadness now. Even if I do not know your whereabouts, I feel sure that the day I seek you in my heart, you will be there. And I know this to be the truth, regardless of what you say.'

Bipradas smiled and, as in the case of his son, he gave her no answer.

***

The car rolled away.

GLOSSARY

Babu	A gentleman, also used as a suffix after a man's name as a mark of respect
Baba	Father
Barda	Elder brother
Barababu	Senior-most male head of a family
Beimashai	Father or uncle-in-law of a son or a daughter
Benthakrun	Mother or aunt-in-law of a son or daughter
Baisakh	First month of the Bengali calendar
Bhadra	Fifth month of the Bengali calendar
Brahmo sect	A new monotheistic faith propagated by Ram Mohun Roy in the 1830s
Boudie	Wife of an elder brother
Bouma	Wife of a son
Dada	Elder brother or an elder male cousin
Didi	Elder sister or an elder female cousin
Dakhsineshwar	A much venerated Hindu temple near Calcutta
Ekadashi	Eleventh day of the full moon or the new moon, traditionally observed as the fast days by Hindu widows
Gita	A holy book of Hindus
Jagadhatri	A Hindu female deity

Kailashnath and Mansarovar	Holy Hindu pilgrimage near India/Tibet border
Kaka	Uncle, father's younger brother
Lathi	Stick
Masi	Aunt, mother's sister
Mejdi	Elder sister, second in rank in seniority
Thakurma	Grandmother, father's mother
Thakurpo	Younger brother of husband
Zamindar	Landlord

About the Author

Sarat Chandra Chattopadhyay (1876–1938) was an illustrious Bengali novelist and short story writer of the early 20th century. Many of his stories narrate the lives, tragedies, and struggles of the village people and the contemporary social practices that prevailed in Bengal. His writing matured at a time when the national movement was gaining momentum together with an awakening of social consciousness.

Sensitive and daring, his novels captivated the hearts and minds of innumerable readers both in Bengal and the rest of India. His best known novels include *Palli Samaj* (1916), *Choritrohin* (1917), *Devdas* (1917), *Nishkriti* (1917), *Srikanta* (1917), *Datta* (1918), *Griha Daha* (1920), and *Sesh Prashna* (1929). Many of his stories were adopted for well-crafted and popular films in Bengali and Hindi languages for many years, extending even to the 21st century.

He remains the most popular, most translated, most adapted, and the most plagiarized Indian author of all time.

About the Translator

Sukhendu Ray qualified as a Chartered Accountant from England in 1950, and after working for a British multinational group Guest Keen Williams Ltd., he retired as that company's Managing Director and Chief Executive. Post retirement, along with his professional assignments, he took to translating Bengali literature into English. Included in his published translated works are: *The Winged Horse* (OUP), *Three Novellas: Three long stories by Rabindranath Tagore* (OUP), *Thakurmar Jhuli* by Dakshinaranjan Mitra Majumder (OUP), *Chirakumar Sabha: The Bachelors Club* by Rabindranath Tagore (OUP), a number of verse and prose pieces for the *Selected Writings for Children* by Rabindranath Tagore (OUP), *Travels to Persia and Iraq in 1932* by Rabindranath Tagore (Viswa-Bharati), *Datta* by Sarat Chandra Chattopadhyay (Rupa), *Chokher Bali* by Rabindranath Tagore (Rupa), and *The Many Worlds Of Sarala Devi—A Diary* by Sarala Devi Chaudhurani (Social Science Press).

ENG-25

74268